In the Company of Dragons

Book One of the Guardian Chronicles

By

B. Johnson

Acknowledgements

I dedicate this book to my biggest fan club, my parents, my children, and Nadine and Shawna, for without their support I wouldn't have been able to do this. To a dear friend, Breanna Whitehouse, who always read everything I sent her way and wasn't afraid to tell me it sucked. And to my beta-group readers, Carissa & Trevor Weeks, Wayson Cumiford, Kalleigh Wagner, & Madison Gates who cemented the fact my story was worth sharing. Thank you!

And to the reader, thank you for taking this journey with me.

"No, I would not want to live in a world without dragons, as I would not want to live in a world without magic, for that is a world without mystery, and that is a world without faith."

R.A. Salvatore, *Streams of Silver*

Table of Contents

1. Guardians

2. Alliance

3. Rumors

4. A Fool's Errand

5. Transformations

6. Blood Lust

7. Annihilation

8. Heartache

9. Deliverance

10. Loss

11. Reunited

12. Deceptions

13. Family Business

14. Well Laid Plans

15. When Legends Fall Short

16. Friendship

17. Liberation

18. What Evil This Way Comes….

19. Dilemma

20. Unexpected

20. Unexpected

21. Weakness and Strength

22. Protection

23. Class Dismissed

24. A New Life

1. Guardians

The sun, bright and full, slowly stretched its warm rays across the valley below. The morning's dew, on the roof tops of several make shift huts made from caked mud and straw, glistened as the light crept over the small village; its warmth sure to awaken some of the inhabitants. A range known for its rough terrain but lush landscape was tucked into the southwest side of the Liastreil Mountains and was a perfect place for the Guardians to live. Only in the times that they would stumble upon a place so lacking in what the rest of the fey realm would consider desirable living space would they actually have a chance to call a place home for longer than two moons' time. Faineth and her family were among such a clan.

Deemed as some of the most controversial people in Ethreal, the Guardians, or as most the fey folk liked to call them, Travelers, were not accepted into the mainstream of society. Thought of as evil witch gypsies that dabbled in blood and black magic, most of the fey world shunned them, leaving them to a life as nomadic outcasts. Faineth's people did have a magic like no other, but not the evil sort they had been labeled with, instead one of benefit and healing. They did use dragon's blood for some of the spells they performed, but mostly their talents didn't venture much past that of a humble Hedge Witch, helping with midwifery needs and cures for ailments, such as unsightly warts or fevers or anything in between. There were a few though, Faineth being one of them, whose skills did excel the clan's average talents.

Being only seventeen years old, Faineth was wise beyond her years. Considered a bit of a misfit within her own clan, she was not really interested in the social ways of their clan life, and this allowed her ample time to exceed in many of the ways of her people. Outside of her immediate family, there was nothing more important to her than the dragons. Learning their ways, their routines, and their life was all that mattered to the young Guardian. Where most of the younger folk in her clan enjoyed socializing and wasting time, Faineth was more about getting ahead in her courses and learning as much as she could.

The true label of their kind, Dragon Guardians, was something given to them. Not a self- given title by any means and it was not given by the fey folk of Ethreal, but by the dragons themselves, centuries before Faineth was even born. There were many, many legends as to how this happened, but only one was true and only the Guardians themselves knew it. The dragons picked their people, because their hearts were a perfect match; noble and true, loving and magical.

The rays of the sun peeked through the window and danced across her face, causing her to awaken fully. She soon realized it had the same effect on her slumber mate, Willow, as she stretched out her wings fully to absorb some of the morning heat. The tiny dragon allowed her tail to uncoil and it hit Faineth's leg behind her knee.

"Ouch, Willow! Be careful!" Faineth snapped, but smiled before the small creature took it to heart. Willow made a low, vibrating sound in her throat; much like a cat's purring would sound and coiled her tail quickly in response.

"Thank you, little one. Whatever should we accomplish today, hmm?" she spoke with a smile, softly rubbing the underside of the dragon's chin, which only made the purring sound grow deeper; a sound of pure pleasure for a dragon.

Faineth stretched out her toes as she sat up and hung her legs over her make shift bed of old tattered blankets, meal sacks and strategically placed twigs. The life of a Dragon Guardian was not one of wealth and luxury. It was actually quite the opposite. Made of caution and discipline and above all, the ability to stay hidden, the life of a Guardian could only be described as prudent.

Though her people were many, they were scattered and only a few of the outside Fey world were let in and only then when necessary. This practice ensured her people's safety and above all else, peace.

Faineth rose from her bed and Willow quickly followed, climbing the back of her skirts, burrowing under her hair and finally resting on what the little creature considered her spot, Faineth's shoulders. She wrapped her body much like one would wear a scarf and sighed.

"You know, it won't be much longer that I will not be able to carry you around like this. You are growing faster than I realized. What are you now, five, maybe six, stones?" Faineth teased and Willow nudged her chin with the tip of her nose. Willow, catching the smell of something good, climbed off Faineth's shoulder and scurried out of the room before Faineth could protest.

"Oh, well, don't let me keep you," she laughed, but caught the smell herself and quickly grabbed her boots, hoisting them on one at a time as she hopped out of the room almost as fast as her dragon had exited seconds before. Warm food was always a great way to start a day and as far as she was concerned, her mother was the best cook in the entire Fey realm.

"Faineth!" her mother, Olorin, shouted out without looking up, just as Faineth entered the kitchen. She was bent over the fire, stirring the morning's meal.

It was a simple kitchen, made up of the basic necessities. It had a sink for washing made of an old metal tub her father had formed for her mother at the blacksmith's that sat upon a stack of properly positioned rocks. Her father had also built her mother long, narrow tables that he then propped up against the walls to give her mother some work space, which she filled with different sized jars of spoons, herbs, and spices. Several different sized pots hung from above the fireplace that was in the opposite corner of the table, as well as meats and fruits that were drying by the heat of the fire. It was nothing fancy, but it was the most comfortable room in the house.

"What, Mama dear?" she shouted in reply, jokingly, causing her mother to jump and almost drop the spoon in the pan of whatever was creating the wonderful smell, as well as hit her head on the inside top of the hearth.

"Faineth Seeri R'yor! If I didn't think that dragonling of yours wouldn't bite off the hand I'm stirrin' with, I'd soon blister that back side of yours for nearly stealing my heart from my chest!" her mother scolded, waving the spoon from the pot in her direction, but soon smiled as she lifted out the pot from over the fire and poured some of the mash into a bowl for her daughter, lovingly placing it in front of her. Olorin then scooped up some and ladled it out into a bowl for Willow. Sweet scents of cinnamon and apple lifted from the bowls and the two wasted no time in devouring it. Olorin placed the pot back over the fire and turned back towards her daughter, taming some of Faineth's long, thick, wavy hair as she watched her gulp down the food almost mimicking the dragon without trying to. Her mother watched them both, glancing back and forth, plaiting Faineth's locks and comparing the two silently.

"One would think you were raised by them and not me, by looking at ya," she said, pointing to Willow.

"Hum?" Faineth stopped what she was doing long enough to see what her mother meant, straightened herself up, and repositioned the spoon in her hand, making sure her pinky finger was as straight as a tree branch; she continued to take bites at a slower pace.

"Like this, Mother?" Faineth questioned with a heavy proper sarcasm in her tone.

"Joke now, fool girl, but you'll no be getting a man to love ya if he can't tell ya apart from Willow," Olorin pulled at the end of her braid in frustration.

"Maybe I don't want a man," Faineth protested with mouth full, rubbing the back of her head. "Maybe I just want to be me. I see how the women who 'get a man' change. They get all weird

10

and home like, completely abandoning their trainings to take care of that man. Most men I know are more of a creature than the dragons, 'cept Ennon and Pa. I would rather stay in my courses and become the best dragon rider, then settle down with one of them."

"Well, you can't go marryin' your brother or your Pa," she scolded her daughter, this time with more meaning than that of a joke between mother and daughter and settled in the chair between the girl and her dragon. "What's so wrong with the idea of giving me some wee little grandbabes someday? I know I sound like a harpy half the time,, but don't discount it forever. Promise me, Faineth. The Shúirí Féile is next month, maybe you should consider going this year?" she asked her voice softer, almost pleading. Her mother was referring to a festival held once a year (in the old language, Shúirí Féile, pronounced 'shoo-eerie fey-isle' meant "engagement festival") where all the young people of the clans would gather in search of a mate. Some would start attending these fairs as early as fourteen years of age, which Faineth thought of as complete idiocy. Her mother had started pushing her to go the day after she turned fourteen. There would never be a day that she would like the idea of being what she considered a 'slave' to a man. Olorin, as far as Faineth was concerned, was one of those women that had given up everything to be with her father.

Looking at her now, one might be able to see that she used to be beautiful, but years of hard labor and tending two children and a husband, had washed that away. Even her flame red hair (which was a characteristic of the women in the clans) used to be the prettiest in all the lands, but now had faded and the wisps of white had all but taken over. It was when she saw her father gaze lovingly at her mother in stolen moments when he thought no one else noticed that Faineth remembered her beauty. His eyes must have been blinded to the change that had taken her soft beauty away, for all that shown in his eyes was surely the desire for what she once had been.

She quickly swallowed the last bite of her breakfast, dropped the spoon in her bowl, and whistled at Willow, who quickly heeded, crawling back in her position of Faineth's neck.

11

"You might have to bother Ennon with that notion, Mamma. I would rather ride a pig than attend the fair or push one of those crying creatures out of my body. Bye! Love you! Wish me luck today!" she rambled as fast as she could, walking out the door, not allowing her mother any more time to argue.

The makeshift village was in it's usually glory, with all the sights and sounds of the morning's business being attended to. She watched as she strolled along, families setting up for market, hanging rows of dried herbs and smoked meats, filling the air with smells that made her question if she truly got enough to eat. Sounds of women pounding out grains into fine flours in large carved out stone bowls and the men from the blacksmith's banging their hammers on red hot steel, gave her an odd sense of belonging. She figured that one would have to be raised with those sounds to fully appreciate them, which she did. Commotions like these always did draw a smile to her face, but hearing the sound of her mother continuing to yell her name inside the little kitchen her mother called home, encouraged her to run the rest of the way to her morning lesson. Willow felt the same and stretched her wings out, lifting from Faineth's shoulders into flight, pulling her hair and scratching her flesh a little in take-off.

"Ahh! You are so fortunate I love you!" she yelled, grabbing her shoulder to access the damage. She drew her hand back and saw blood. Even though it was minimal, it stung. Willow had probably licked her claw to clean it after eating and some of the dragon's venom had now transferred to Faineth's wound, causing the pain she was now feeling. She made a mental note to look for some Dragon Sage on her way.

She had learned a few years back in one of her herbal and botany courses, that Dragon Sage cured all but one dragon's venom, the Black Dragon, and almost instantly. All one had to do was pick it and chew it to a fine pulp within seconds of its leaving the plant and apply it to the wound. If one did exactly that, then it would heal almost immediately and the venom's effects would actually reverse, leaving no trace on its victim that it had happened in the first place. Not even a scar would be left to tell the story.

12

If one could not find Dragon Sage, or not get it chewed and applied to the wound fast enough, depending on the dragon that inflicted the wound, anything from large pus filled blisters for weeks to death could happen to its victim. Faineth could never see that happening because of how obnoxious a weed it was. Besides, dealing with any wound was not in the plans for Faineth today. She had harnessing course and potions to do today and didn't want to miss either. If she passed her harnessing today, her master said he would start her on flying alone the next week. Flying was something she had been looking forward to all year.

She turned down the path to the water, knowing she would find the weed she was looking for more easily there. Clumps of it would grow there at certain times of the year, enough that they would have to pull most of it out to get to the lake itself. Fortunately for her, this was not that time of year, but there would still be enough for her to find. Turning around the last of the large standing boulders on the path and ducking under the last of the large vines that hung in the trees, the lake opened up and she caught sight of a patch of the sage growing near the fresh water spring that fed the lake. This would allow her to take a drink and wash the mornings meal out of her mouth to ensure potency of the weed she was about to chew.

Kneeling down at the spring's edge, Faineth cupped her hands, gathering enough of the water to clean her mouth. She swooshed it around then spit it out then leaned down, dropping her face in the water and gathered up some more to drink. The water was crisp and cold and tasted good. Her shoulder began to sting more, reminding her why she was there.

"Tondendum Reflexio," she said, tracing her fingers in the air. In front of her, hovering just over the water appeared a mirror. It was an odd sort of mirror, not really having sides or a frame, but was more like a piece of the air suddenly had become reflective. This would serve her well to apply the weed concoction she needed for her shoulder. The wound was in a weird spot, making it hard to see without it.

She grabbed a handful of the weed and wasted no time in chewing it up to the desired consistency she would need. The weed actually had a sweet taste to it, much like clover flower in the summer. She pulled her hair over her other shoulder, chewed a little more on the paste and went to examine the scratches, looking back into the mirror. She jumped at the reflection and almost lost her much needed ointment in the grass.

"Ennon…loo wha you amos ded!" she shouted with a mouth full, losing concentration on the spell, causing the mirror to fade. Faineth spit out the paste into her palm and bent down. Her brother took the sage paste from her hand and rubbed it into the wound for her. The pain was subsiding and so was her annoyance at Ennon, but she wasn't letting him off the hook that easily.

"Thanks. Feels better already," she sneered sarcastically at him. Ennon was only a year and a half older than Faineth, but towered over her in height, making him appear much older than he actually was. He was, next to Willow, the most precious being in her world. Not having a clue herself where romance was concerned; Faineth often thought her brother and Father were the perfect example of how a man should be. There were no other boys or men in the village who could measure up to Ennon in her eyes, yet another reason she could never see herself in marriage. It wouldn't be fair for that man to always be compared to her brother. Ennon knew though, that when the right man came along, that man would change her mind, and Faineth would learn why their mother pushed her so hard in that direction.

"I didn't mean to startle you. Glad I was here, though. That's quite the scratch," he said as he quickly rubbed the paste on her shoulder. "Maybe it's time Willow didn't hitch rides on your shoulders anymore? Not like she's getting any smaller."

"I know. Ouch!" she cringed, discovering she wasn't completely pain free yet.

"Sorry, here." Ennon finished up applying it and rubbed his hands clean in the lake. "I just don't want this to be considered the smallest mark that dragon leaves on my sister."

"She's not just a dragon, she's beautiful and rare and loving! You are just jealous, brother, that one of these magnificent creatures has not attached itself to you the same way," Faineth scolded, sounding like an authority on them, looking curiously in the sky for the dragon she just made excuses for.

"She's over with the Wyrmryns so you can stop looking," he answered, knowing what she was asking in her mind. "May she always be worthy of your affection and loyalty, little sister."

She stood up, adjusting her shirt back into place and smiled at her brother.

"That's where you have it wrong, Ennon. May I live up to the worthiness she deserves," Faineth said, grabbing the sleeve of Ennon's shirt, pulling him back in the direction of fields where their lessons of the day would be.

2. Alliance

Ennon and Faineth, along with their parents, were part of the Eastern Clan of Guardians. There were six known clans in Ethreal, the Eastern, Western, Northern and Southern, as well as the Under Dwellers and the Ocean Clans. Each of the different clans was the caregivers to specific dragon species. There were sixty eight species of dragons in total and their characteristics and needs to survive were the determining factors of which clan they dwelled with. Faineth's clan cared for the highest number of dragons, twenty species total.

Each species of dragon was quite unique from one another and most lived very harmoniously together, but there were a few in which that wasn't the case. In the Eastern Clan, Land Wyrmryns and Gweiths play together as if they were from the same egg, which was quite peculiar if you knew them. Land Wyrmryns for one were not what they appeared. On the outside, they were very large and very intimidating. Reddish orange in color, they appeared to be painted by the fire of the sun. But they were quite lovely creatures, easy to get along with, the most loyal of their breed, and fiercely protective of all the clans. They only had one odd characteristic. They were very afraid of a common snake, which explains the peculiar friendship with the Gweith Dragon.

Gweith Dragons looked like a large snake with small wings. They were almost silent in movement and loved to manipulate the enemy in a game of hide and seek. The only problem for said enemy is that once a Gweith has determined you as such, it is already too late. They will trick you into believing you have escaped, when in reality, they are right behind you, or in front, if you are silly enough to take your eyes off the road ahead.

For the Ocean clan, things weren't as easy. The clan only had two species of dragons that they cared for, the mischievous Laqueous and the ever dutiful Marine Wyvern. The Laqueous, the dragon version of a young male wood pixie, with its trickery and folly, was the opposite of the ever watchful, ever steadfast protection of the Marine Wyvern. When the two tried to live in the same stretches of the Ocean, they would often fight, causing huge tidal waves and whirlpools that often grew so massive it would cross over into the human realm. Because of this, the clan had to break into two groups and live apart, doing their best to keep these two dragons from crossing paths. Unfortunately, they weren't always successful.

The dragons that belonged to the Under Dwellers were the ones that scared Faineth the most. While there were only six species belonging to this group, the only one that mattered as far as she was concerned, was the Black Dragon, called the most feared of all dragons. Faineth was grateful that she was not part of that clan. As much as she loved to learn about the other species, the Black Dragon was not one she knew much about. She knew they were the largest of all dragons and rumored to have a heart as black as their skin and that was enough for her. That alone was scary enough to halt her insatiable curiosity where dragons were concerned and she wasn't alone. Most outside of that clan decided a long time ago that visiting was better if they waited for the Under Dwellers to come to them.

Willow was one of the last Great Whites. There was rumored to be only five left in all of Ethreal and the fact that Faineth had her at all was a shear miracle, as they were rogue dragons. They did not live, nor bother with, any of the six clans. Some of the clans' folk even thought they were the Maker's dragons and therefore could not be owned by any created thing.

The little Guardian had found her in egg form on one of her countless terrain lessons. She had strayed off the path, something Faineth did quite often and got into trouble for, but it never stopped the next exploration from happening. The day she found

Willow, she had entered her group, already bored with the idea of studying paths and trails.

She knew the land, like it was a part of her, so a detour was inevitable. Once she saw the opportunity to leave, she took it. Running along a smaller, overgrown path, she stumbled on some rocks hidden under the brush. She fell almost flat out in front of her, hitting her head on another rock covered by a patch of lily moss, but when she went to see the size of the rock because of the pain it had inflicted, it turned out to be a dragon's egg instead.

"Well, this is a very odd place for you to be, aye, little one?" Faineth said rubbing her forehead, then lifted the egg up with the utmost respect, getting a better look at it. She glanced around curiously, looking to see if mama dragon was close. It was like no other egg she had ever seen and no evidence of the female that had laid it, so she hid it in her pack and quickly ran back home, faking a stomach ache to get out of her courses for the rest of the day. She knew her mother would be busy with the daily chores and not fuss with her much, giving Faineth plenty of time to study her father's old books about the creatures.

Arien, Faineth's father, kept most of his books and scrolls in a smaller space in the back of their home. He often said it was far enough out of the way to study without too much distraction, but not too far to miss the goings on of the house. She always marveled at the way her father could focus on his work, but seem to know everything that was happening around him. She was glad he was hunting today, so that she too might go about her business of finding the right information without being disturbed, or at least she could be hopeful.

Faineth eventually found what she was looking for, but it was not to be found amongst her father's books. It took months to find and to her surprise, another clansman to help her find it. Once a year, they would hold a gathering, where all the clans would get come together and with their clan having been in the same spot for many years as well as occupying the most land, it was always held in their village. As many times as she could get away with it, Faineth would stay behind to listen to the Elders of each clan, fully knowing that half the things worth knowing in life happened after their opening ceremonial meetings dispersed, allowing the clan folk to mingle, eat, shop, and spin tall tales of battles and breeding. This would not be the first time she had eavesdropped on one of their conversations.

The Elders would wait until they were alone and then gather together in a much smaller circle, one that kept out other, lesser clansmen. She had discovered a notch in the clay of the main building, almost directly above them, on one of her adventures, which she fit effortlessly into, making the perfect hiding place. While most were filing out of the large clay and wood reed hut, she used the noise as a distraction to climb into her spot and nestle her and her egg, before the room fell quiet.

"It pays to be small, huh, little one," she whispered, smiling down at her treasure.

At first, the older clansmen mostly drank and talked about the weather and other boring, silly things, making Faineth wonder why she stuck around to listen this time, but just before she was about to nod off, words from one of the stories being told below, clicked…White Dragon.

She had never heard of the species before and she thought she had known them all. She looked down at her egg that she had diligently kept safe for the past fourteen full moons, almost giving up hope that the time to meet her new friend was close, as most of the dragons only took around ten full moons to hatch. This egg was different though, not only in color but in size, shape, and texture. It was a very light iridescent gray, almost resembling dull silver and slightly smaller. The texture was smooth like glass which was odd because it had a definite scale pattern.

Faineth also noticed that once in a while it would look like water, clear and clean, but you could not see the dragon within its shell. Before now, she had started to believe it wasn't a dragon's egg at all, but possibly some magical tool or seed.

19

"Where did you say they found the dragon, Sogan?" asked one of the elders to another.

"We found her in the Eastern Regions, quite close to the fields of Rhemmon," answered the elder named Sogan.

Faineth gasped, but quickly covered her mouth. Luckily the Elders were, well, elderly and didn't hear her. She knew they would stop talking about it if she was discovered. The fields of Rhemmon were where she and the other younger clansmen learned their art. It was the field she was walking around on the paths that she had ventured off the day she found the egg.

"She was already dead when we had reached her, but my son found evidence that she had birthed her egg before her last breath. We were not successful at finding the egg. My belief is that one of the other five took it with them."

Other five? Faineth was confused and looked down at her egg, softly rubbing it with her thumb. This egg only has five living family members, she thought to herself. It was exactly how she herself felt most of the time, regardless to the size of her clan. The shell started to warm like it always did when she caressed it and Faineth cradled it closer to her. The elders continued to talk, pulling her back into the conversation.

"Well, I do hope you did exactly what was expected and buried the creature in accordance to the laws," shouted an Elder she recognized as Vorin, Lord of the Under Dwellers. *The man gave Faineth shivers as he spoke.* *"You are quite aware of what would happen if you did not."*

"Of course we did, Vorin, preparations were made immediately," Sogan said, in defense.

"The last thing any of us want is to have the Maker upset, Vorin, and I'm sure Sogan and his men feel the same way. No need to question his law keeping skills," spoke Alatar, the Lord of the Eastern clan. *"Besides, Sogan was my guest that day. He came only by my request."*

"Just making sure that we don't have another..." Vorin started to say something but he was cut off.

"The battle of Enot was well over three thousand moons ago, Vorin, and I think I speak for everyone here when I say that we have all done our part to prevent that from ever happening again," Neisa, one of the twin Elders of the Ocean clan, stated in her soft spoken yet authoritative way and it made everyone in the hut jump a bit, including Faineth, as none of them had heard her enter. Faineth quickly looked around, knowing Sena would be close.

"Yes, Vorin," Sena spoke with a snake like hiss, as she walked out behind the shadow of her twin sister. "You always assume the worst, don't you, my friend?" she hissed again as she circled the men in the room, weaving in between each of them, setting the whole room on edge. "I see you have saved me and my sister a seat as always," she added with heavy sarcasm.

Faineth had never seen the elders move as fast as they did at that moment, practically fumbling over each other to find the twins a place to sit within the circle. Where the Elders of the land clans were older and wrinkled, the twins were youthful and very beautiful. It was said to be the gift of the waters. It kept them from aging past a certain time. She wondered too, if that was the reason why their red hair always looked as if it were on fire. Though they were equally beautiful, Neisa was more the elegant beauty in every way, from the way she looked to the way she carried herself. Sena, on the other hand, was much more of a wild beauty. Her clothes, her hair, and even her speech defined chaos and mischief, making her a perfect Guardian for the Laqueous. It struck Faineth in a funny way to see the other Elders fuss over the women so much as if they were the Queens of the clans and the rest were the faithful subjects.

"Forgive us, Sisters," spoke Vorin, in a more delicate manner than before. He bowed slightly towards them, lifting his eyes to see Neisa. It was also rumored that he had been in love with her since the first day they met, which was quite some time considering they were both very, very old. Faineth choked back a

giggle, for she thought Sena was a much more perfectly suited match to Vorin, the man in charge of the Black Dragons.

The twins sat down, across from each other so that they could be literally in the middle of the conversation and things continued. The men told the twins all that they had been discussing, as a sign of respect. Faineth thought it was to ensure them that they had in fact had not been excluded in the first place.

"I'm sure the Lords were talking about a much more interesting topic than that of the weather, or trainings of the youth," Sena hissed again annoyance, as she glared at the old men surrounding her.

"And I'm sure that they are just about to get to that part, dear sister," chimed in Neisa. Faineth really like Neisa; her mannerisms reminded her of her own mother, soft and sweet, yet very to-the-point. They both had a way of delivering bad news or upholding the laws with a spoonful of sweet berry nectar, in other words, to the point without breaking the person's spirit in the act.

"Yes, Milady, we were actually discussing a very important matter when you and your dear sister joined us," Gwaydden, Lord of the Southern clan, reassured her gracefully.

"Please, Gwaydden, don't let us stop you," hissed Sena, her dark eyes seeming to pierce right through his heart.

"No, Milady," he said, with a sort of shy way that made Faineth take notice. Old folk were sometimes such odd characters, she thought to herself.

"A White Dragon was discovered," Gwaydden started to tell, but the gasp from Sena stopped him from finishing.

"A White Dragon?" she questioned, looking over at Neisa. "Are you sure?"

"Yes, Milady, we are quite sure," answered Sogan.

22

"Where is it now? How close did you actually get to it, oh, I'm so jealous, is it gone?" she asked the questions almost faster than Faineth could keep up and she saw the excitement all over Sena's face. Her wicked smile gave Faineth flesh bumps.

"I'm sorry, Sena, we did not find the creature alive," Alatar broke the news to her, looking at the floor as he said the words.

The room got quiet, too quiet, and Faineth was too involved in the conversation below to notice she had edged out of her little hiding spot enough to cause some of the clay to scrape off and send dust particles softly floating down to the edge of where the Elders sat. Still, it seemed only one took notice.

"The real question is not whether you have properly buried the great dragon, but how much did you say about this matter not realizing you have an audience," Neisa asked diplomatically.

It took a few moments for what she said to actually make sense to the others and they started to look around the room. Neisa lifted her hand to her mouth, placing her first finger over her lips as to silence the others and then pointed straight up to Faineth with a smile. Faineth's heart nearly stopped.

"Come, little one, come and join us, won't you?" she asked as if Faineth would have her very own seat and be as welcomed as the rest of them were.

She froze, not really knowing what to do and clutched the egg tighter to her skirts. Sena stood up and made an impatient sound and raised her hand in the direction of Faineth.

"Incidere ex supero," she hissed and Faineth, against every ounce of her will, was removed from the little hole and floated down to hover directly in front of Sena.

"Hi?" was all the young clan girl could manage as she stared at Sena, whose glare caused the flesh bumps that were already there to grow twice in size. Sena hissed and dropped her finger and Faineth dropped the rest of the way with a thump to the *floor. She desperately fiddled with her skirt, trying to conceal the egg from them as Neisa stood and walked towards them and stood to the right of her twin.*

"I know you, don't I?" she asked, smiling at Faineth.

Faineth had no clue what she was talking about, as she only ever saw the Twin Lords from a distance.

"You're Olorin's daughter, aren't you?" she asked.

The sound of Faineth's mothers name caused her to look at Neisa strangely. How in all of Ethreal did her mother not happen to mention them knowing each other?

"Ya--yes, Milady...yes..." she managed to stutter out.

"I knew it! My, you have really grown! I haven't seen you since you were but a wee thing," Neisa said, grabbing Faineth's shoulders twisting her around to get a better look at her. The motion caused Faineth to drop the egg and it rolled across the floor and stopped at the feet of Vorin.

"What's this?" he asked. He bent down to pick up the egg and as he stood, the rest of the room finally saw what he was talking about. The egg's once transparent blue gray color instantly dulled to pale silver and took on the appearance of stone, as if it had withered at his touch. The group gasped and once again, the room fell hauntingly quiet.

"I know what that is," hissed Sena. "Question is, what are you doing with it, child?"

"The egg... it was not taken by the others, after all..." stated Sogan.

"We should, no, we must take this to Mount Garasi, without hesitation! We must return this egg to the Maker before we all feel his wrath!" shouted Vorin.

"We will not do any such thing, Vorin," Neisa spoke softly but to the point, showing some of that berry nectar. "Don't you

24

understand? This is the first time anything of this nature has happened. This egg, this amazing, wonderful egg, has chosen a keeper. This special girl is to take care of this egg and her alone."

Faineth looked at her in shock, as did the rest of the group, including Sena.

"What are you talking about, sister? Why her?" Sena asked Neisa, with zero trust in her voice.

"Dear Sena, why not her? Have we as Guardians ever asked that question before? Why did the Laqueous pick you? Wait, don't answer that," she teased and it seemed to help lighten the tension in the room a little, but Sena made a sound towards her twin that scolded her for the comment. Neisa stepped closer to Faineth and cupped her chin in her hand. She lifted Faineth's face up so their eyes could meet.

"Why not her?" she whispered again and smiled. "Vorin, it seems you have something that belongs to this little one. Can you please bring it over to her, before it senses the loss of her warmth?"

Vorin jolted out of his trance and looked at the egg as if it would explode in his hands, rushing over to give it back before it had a chance to prove his theory right. He gingerly handed it to Faineth and quickly stepped away. Faineth had never seen anything like it and looked at her egg more curiously than before, which was changing back to the appearance she was used to.

"Now, let's you and I take a little walk, shall we?" Neisa asked Faineth, pulling her into the safety of her arm, leading her out of the hut. One advantage of being as beautiful as the twin Elders were, was that no one questioned their motives, at least not at first. Not without time to process what had just happened.

"Sena," she called out to her sister, who was looking equally puzzled as the rest of the Lords, "Please fill me in on the rest of the evening's business when I return? If Faineth is half the company of her mother, I may be awhile."

"But-" Sena tried to argue.

"Thank you, sister," Neisa said and the conversation was over. The two of them left too quickly for any of the others to dispute her decision.

~*~

Faineth walked alongside her brother, heading in the direction of the field remembering that night she had spent talking with Neisa. It would be a memory she would cherish forever. They really didn't talk about the egg or what made Faineth as special as Neisa had led on, but rather she wanted to know all about her lessons and her life's dreams. Faineth had no problem sharing all her desires to be the best dragon maiden the clans had ever seen and Neisa never once laughed at her, or made her feel as if any of it was unattainable. If anything, she complimented her on her achievements and marveled in how much she had learned in such a short period of time. She had mentioned her great grandmother as well and said that Faineth reminded Neisa of her. Faineth knew little of her, but thought it must have been something special if Neisa thought to mention the similarity. All in all, her new friend made her feel like she may be gifted and that she was right to want to learn as much as she could. She was even kinder, more wonderful than Faineth had first thought. It saddened her to think she hadn't had a chance to see Neisa since that night, but the memories of it kept her close at all times.

3. Rumors

"There you two are, been lookin' for you all morning!" shouted Blaen, a friend of the siblings as he ran up to them on the trail to their lessons.

"Well, you found us, Blaen, now what are you going to do with us?" Faineth teased. Blaen ruffled her hair much like an older brother would and smiled. He in fact was best friends with her brother Ennon, but he had a soft spot for Faineth, as well. Not in a romantic sort of way, not even close. He had three brothers himself, so he sort of adopted Faineth as the sister he never got in life. The children in the clan would tease that since Faineth had Ennon and Blaen watching out for her, none of the boys in the clan would dare approach her come matching time, which suited her just fine.

"I'm not gonna do anythen!" he teased. "But I am gonna tell ya the lessons have been canceled today, something about an emergency Elders meeting. Pfft, I don't care if it was to wash their backsides; it means freedom today for us, aye?" Blaen smiled as he delivered the news to his dear friends.

Faineth, even though disappointed she would be missing out in her harnessing lessons, immediately thought of Neisa.

"Well, now, that changes things up a bit. Let's say we head over to Widow's Lake? We aren't far from home yet and it would only take a few moments to detour and grab our poles," Ennon suggested. Blaen beamed as he loved the idea, but Faineth stumbled for excuses to get out of going with them.

"Actually, I think I'm going to see if Mama needs some help," she tried out, but even to her, it sounded ridiculous.

"What? Since when have you chosen chores over fishing?" questioned her brother.

"Well, I need to... practice some incantations before tomorrow's courses," she tried again.

"Well, I never thought in a million moons that the little wonder named Faineth ever needed to practice her spells. Aren't you more of the wing it and pray kind a girl?" questioned Blaen, half teasing, half truthful.

"What's really going on, Faineth? We aren't falling for the excuses today," Ennon scolded.

"Fine, I'm going to see if I can see her and neither of you two is going to stop me from trying," she blurted out with as much authority as she could muster.

The boys turned and smiled at each other, as if sharing some secret and Blaen ruffled the top of Faineth's head again.

"You are gonna get yourself caught again, you know that right?" he asked.

"Well, maybe not this time. Willow is nowhere to be found," Ennon said, searching the skies for her little dragon.

The boys laughed, but Faineth only snickered at them.

"Laugh all you want! It's not like I'm going to be spying again or anything. I just want to see her and show her Willow. She hasn't seen her since she was an egg."

"Fine, but if you get caught, we were not here, we did not say it was okay for you to go, and we know nothin'," Blaen stated, protecting the boys from fault.

"I never saw you, you had no idea where I was going, and you are completely stupid, got it! Thanks!" she said, running off before they could argue. The boys laughed it off and turned in the direction of their homes to gather their needed fishing supplies.

It didn't take long for Faineth to find her little cohort. Willow was right where Ennon had said and with a couple of whistles she was flying low, right above Faineth's head.

"I can't wait for her to meet you!" Faineth shouted up at Willow and the little dragon reacted with a barrel roll, straightening out while upside down.

"Show off," she laughed and Willow turned up right and let out a bellow followed by fire. Faineth laughed. She loved how it seemed Willow knew everything she was saying.

It took less than she figured for the pair to get to where they were going. Faineth slowed down just as they got to the outskirts of the gathering place of the Elders, so she and Willow wouldn't be immediately spotted. Spying wasn't her plan today, but she didn't want to look like she was up to something either and rushing in would draw unwanted attention.

They stopped at the edge of the clearing where the meeting was about to begin. There was a greater number of people there than she had expected. The way Blaen had explained it; she thought it was just the Elders getting together, but this was much bigger. Many of the clan members were there, as well as some of the Fey Folk. She spotted her parents, across the way, standing in front of one of the small huts and when her mother saw her, she waved Faineth over with her hand.

"Now, mama wants to see me and there are far too many out there that wouldn't necessarily welcome you here right now, Willow, so you are going to have to stay here, okay?" she said, rubbing Willow under the chin.

The little dragon let out what sounded like a whimper and dropped her head.

"I thought you might act like that. Here," said Faineth, pulling out a special treat for Willow. She held out a large piece of dried boar's hide, something dragons thought was a delicacy and Willow gladly accepted it and knowing it would take a while to get through it, Faineth wasn't worried that Willow would leave before she returned.

She turned and darted in and out of the towns people, finally reaching where her parents were talking about something with one of the aids to the Elder Alatar. By the expressions on their faces, it looked pretty important. Her quick movements caught her father's eye, which only made his look of concern deepen.

"Faineth! What are you doing here?" questioned her father, sternly.

"I came to show Neisa Will-" she started to answer him, but was stopped short, as he raised his hand, palm out, making it impossible for her to finish her sentence.

"There isn't an excuse that you could conjure up right now that I will accept. You need to leave and join your brother for the afternoon. You shouldn't be here now child."

"But Father, I wanted to show Neisa Willow," she tried to argue.

"Not today! Now, no more of this debate. Neisa will be around another time to meet the dragon, Faineth. Now is not the time," her father spoke, his voice letting her know there was no more room for argument.

Faineth's father, Arien, was not a man to argue with for long. He had a gentle heart when it came to his family, but when it was a matter of business and rules to be followed, he came across harder than stone. She couldn't recall a time when she could reason with him after his mind had been made up.

"Fine," she said, in complete defeat and turned slowly, heading back in the direction of where she had left Willow. "But I'm not a child anymore," she yelled back at her parents, but they had already returned to the conversation they had been in. She sighed and turned back around. She didn't like the idea of coming all this way and not see Neisa, so she quickly came up with a new plan.

As soon as she cleared the building and was no longer visible by either of her parents, she ran and snuck around the back side of the huts, peering through the windows until she could find the one Neisa was in. Thinking that the meeting wasn't all that important, Faineth planned on getting Neisa to follow her back to where she left Willow. Surely, the Elder wouldn't be missed with how many people were there. Finally, after looking around to make sure she wasn't being watched, she slowly lifted her head up to peer through the small window in the back. The room was filled with important looking people that seemed to be in a very serious debate. She quickly looked around the room, without really listening to what was being said, but once again, Neisa was not there. Faineth turned and leaned back against the wall, slightly puzzled at the whereabouts of her friend.

She rested her head against the clay of the hut and voices in the room raised enough that it made her turn and look inside again.

"I'm sure you are mistaken, Roanus. We haven't seen Belamros since the last gathering," spoke Simeon, an aide to Alatar, Lord of the Eastern Clans.

"Well, someone must have seen him. He left word that this was where he was headed," answered Roanus, The King's brother. Belamros, the man they were talking about, was the other brother to the King, the Lord of the North and hand to the King.

"Are you accusing us of lying, Roanus?" asked another clansman.

Roanus, a very large, muscular elf, turned towards the clansmen who had asked.

"What I am saying is that my brother, the hand to your King, left word with us that he was coming here to be changed, some eight days ago. Now, the last time I heard, it doesn't take

31

eight days to do a changing, now does it?" he asked sharply, but didn't wait for an answer to his question. "So now," he said turning around back towards Alatar, "where is my brother?"

"Roanus, I have no doubt in what you are saying, but you must know, we have not seen nor heard from Belamros. If we had, we would be happy to bring you to him," Alatar stated, sounding very diplomatic, but it only angered Roanus more.

"If you are unwilling to help, then you will be willing to allow my men to search every forsaken hut in your clan, top to bottom."

Faineth looked at Alatar, whose expression changed instantly. Why didn't this elf believe her Elder? She reached up to hear and see better, when she felt the soft touch of a hand on her shoulder. Turning around she saw that it was Neisa.

"And to what do we owe the pleasure of your presence at yet another meeting of very important nature, my sweet Faineth?" Neisa asked in more of a reprimanding tone than that of pure acquisition.

"I was actually looking for you, Miss Neisa," Faineth stuttered out nervously. "I heard you were here and I wanted you to meet Willow."

"Ahh, well, how about we go and meet her now, shall we?" she asked, pulling Faineth down off her perch, so the rest of the meeting would remain private. But Faineth found herself wanting to listen to the rest of what was being said in the hut, more than she wanted to introduce Willow to Neisa and stayed firmly planted where she stood.

"Why are they saying all those things? Do they really think he is here?" Faineth asked.

"Willow is waiting for us, dear, let's leave the men to talk of their business, while we go attend to ours, alright?" Neisa said with softness, yet her tone was definite. The answer was no and no argument would sway her. Faineth gave up her pursuit and after a

32

few seconds of silent debate, she agreed, turning with Neisa and heading in the direction she had last left Willow in.

"Changing" as the men had called it, was the art of changing an otherworldly of any species into a human, or vice versa, changing a human into an otherworldly, although Faineth had never witnessed nor heard of the latter ever happening. She had, though, heard of and had even mastered the art of, changing fairy folk into humans. Part of why she earned the reputation and the teasing from her friends and clan's folk her age, of being the wonder witch. It usually took those many years to be able to learn it, let alone master it, and that was if they even could and Faineth did both in under seven moons.

The two walked side by side back to the little white dragon in a manner Faineth thought a bit odd. It was almost as if Neisa was ready for her to turn around and run back to the hut (which Faineth had no intention of doing) and her arm was around her shoulder without really touching her. None the less, it was very curious, very curious indeed, thought Faineth. Grownups were silly creatures, she was now convinced. What they didn't want the younger ones knowing, they tried very hard to hide, cover up so to speak, but what they didn't realize is it just made it all that more interesting to find out. Neisa's behavior at this moment was a perfect example.

Her desire was to have her little dragon meet the woman who had kept them together a few years ago. But now, her curiosity was back, outweighing her previous plans and Neisa's actions were to blame. What was so important, or urgent about Roanus and his brother? And why was he so sure he was here and the clans were hiding him?

"Neisa," Faineth said, looking up at her.

"Yes, child?" she answered softly, but still sounding anxious.

"Has someone been…hurt?" she asked hesitantly.

"Why would you ask that question, Faineth?"

33

"It's just that those men back there were arguing and that one man, Roanus, I think that was his name, well, he accused our clan of hiding that other man he was talking about," Faineth rambled.

"I see you are not going to let this go, are you?" Neisa said as she walked along, not looking down at Faineth as she asked. Her smile was as mischievous as the question.

"It's not really in my nature to, Milady," Faineth admitted. It made Neisa laugh out loud.

"No? Mine either little one, mine either."

"It just doesn't make sense. Why would they think things like that and why haven't I heard about his visit?"

"Well, that is a mystery, isn't it? I'm not really sure why you didn't hear about it. Maybe Belamros didn't want many to know; maybe he came here to one of your clansmen privately. As far as why his brother is accusing the clan of hiding him, well, all I can say to that is that men do strange things in times of desperation. Things I have never been able to make sense of anyways."

"Do you think he is here?" Faineth asked Neisa reluctantly. "Do you think he is in danger?"

"Danger? Here?" she let out a laugh, but it didn't fool Faineth. She could tell something, like fear, hid behind it.

Neisa saw the look on Faineth's face and decided that getting back to Willow was the best thing to do right now and quickly stopped the inquisition.

"I don't really have the answers you seek, Faineth, but what I do know is that Roanus is a man who cannot be trusted. I need you to promise me you will stay as far away from him as possible," Neisa almost demanded then added under her breath almost causing Faineth to miss it, "He is not like the rest of his family. I wouldn't be surprised to find out it was all a ruse to gain what he really wants…power." She then straightened up and plastered a fake smile across her face, telling Faineth the discussion was truly over this time. "I'm really anxious to meet Willow. Is she close?"

Faineth furrowed her brows, not wanting it to end, but knew that pushing things now would not only get her into trouble, it would also eliminate the possibility of Willow meeting Neisa and seeing Willow was the real reason she had sought out Neisa in the first place. The excitement for the two to meet returned.

"Yes, Milady, she's right over there," she said pointing in the direction of the little white dragon.

The visit with Neisa and Willow went just as wonderfully as Faineth had expected. It was almost like Willow knew she was the woman who kept her safe with Faineth. She even let Neisa hold her a bit, which made Faineth swell with happiness. The visit was short, with Neisa having to return to the meetings and Faineth contemplated sneaking back to see if she could gather any more information about what was happening, but decided her freedom, with what her father would do if he caught her again, was more important.

She ran all the way home, Willow flying right along with her and made it back in record time, finding her brother and Blaen sitting at the table talking about something important themselves. They stopped discussing whatever it was abruptly as soon as Faineth stepped foot in their small but humble home.

"Don't let me stop ya…," she said to the boys as they looked at her suspiciously. She reached over them, grabbing a slice of bread her mother had made the day before and a piece of thickly sliced cheese, biting into the combo the minute she put them together.

"Where have you been, little lady, and why aren't you where you said you would be?" asked her brother.

"You aren't my father, Ennon, and for your information, I was where I said I would be. I got sent home on account of them talking about some missing family member to the King," she huffed and took another bite, filling her mouth fuller than before.

"Belamros?" asked Blaen. "Aye, they've been talking about him for a few days, now."

"Belamros? Isn't that the Lord of the North, brother and hand to the King?" asked Ennon.

"Ya, that's him, alright! Rumor is he wanted to be human, broke some prearrangement and all. It's quite scandalous!" Blaen smiled as if the story he was telling was the most excited thing to him.

"What are you talking about, Blaen, and why am I just now hearing about it?" Ennon asked, annoyed at his friend.

Blaen sat upright, realizing his mate was not as pleased as he was.

"Oh, um, well, I thought you knew. Sorry, Ennon. It's just rumors; no one has seen any proof of it just of yet. No reason to believe all the silliness of the brother's threats either, it's silly really, all of it," he rambled nervously.

"Threats?" Ennon picked up on the single word. "What are you talking about, threats?"

"It's silly. It's not even true, Ennon, besides, I think I've said enough already. No reason getting everyone worried over nothin'," he said, trying to sugar coat his words.

"I don't think it's nothing, Blaen. Tell me what have you heard? What threats?"

"Okay, well... someone over heard this guy Roanus saying he was going to wipe us all out if we didn't give up his brother to him. Something about him coming here to be changed cause on account he went and fell hard for some human girl and ended his engagement to some other Fey princess or something and if that didn't chap everyone's hide, he hasn't been seen for over a week. See? Silliness!" he laughed nervously.

Faineth and Ennon looked at each other. Faineth swallowed the bite of bread and cheese she had just shoved in her mouth without chewing it. It went down her throat as if she had just tried to swallow a rock and she could feel the hairs on her arms rise like the morning sun. What did wipe us all out mean?

"Blaen, are you sure? That's what is being said? If we don't give up this man, Belamros, then Roanus' men will kill our clan? How in seven moons does he think that's even possible? The dragons will stop them before they reach us," he laughed in response, but Faineth could see the hair on his arms as well.

"Kill us? Is that what wiping out means? Ennon?" Faineth asked, worried.

"Ya, that's what it means, but don't worry, little sister, that's not going to happen," he said softly. He stood and went to Faineth, wrapping his arms around her for comfort.

"Not sure how you will be able to stop it if it does, Ennon," Blaen said without thinking of what it was doing to Faineth. "You and I both know if they want that, they kill the dragons first and then come after us."

"Enough, Blaen!" Ennon shouted, shifting his eyes towards his sister, trying to get Blaen to see the effect it was having on her.

"Oh, sorry, Faineth, I didn't mean to… I'll just go and see you later, okay, Ennon?" Blaen said, scooping up his pack and cloak, bolting for the door before Ennon could stop him.

"Ennon, do you think that part he said about hurting us is real?"

"I'm not sure, Faineth, I'm not sure." Ennon walked over and sat down at the table, tearing off a piece of the bread and eating it nervously while staring out the window.

It was starting to get dark outside and their parents would be coming home soon. Faineth came and sat down in the chair next to him. The light from the candles burning on the table added to the worry in Ennon's eyes. They sat there for quite a while, not really saying anything to each other, just thinking about the supposed rumor. Faineth's fear rose inside of her and her eyes filled with tears before she realized it.

"Ennon," she said softly, but choked on her words.

"Shh. It's going to be okay, Faineth, I promise. You know Blaen; he loves to make up stories and such, there's probably no truth to what he says."

"It is Ennon, it is," she cried.

"What do you mean? Faineth, what do you know?"

"When I went to the meeting spot to find Neisa, half the clan was there including mother and father. That man, Roanus was there to and he was all sorts of mad! He was yelling at Lord Alatar, saying he knew where his brother, Belamros was, accusing him of all sorts of bad things," she rambled through her tears. "He was all kinds of mad, Ennon, all kinds of mad," she repeated, dropping her head in his lap.

Faineth saw Ennon stiffen at her words. Where Blaen was a story teller, Faineth was not and if she could confirm the suspicions, even if only a little, then he knew they were in trouble.

"Well, that changes things, doesn't it?" he said, rubbing her hair. "Changes all kinds of things."

4. A Fool's Errand

The night was long and eerie and the air was thicker than normal at this time of year. Faineth didn't know if it was the weather or the fact that she felt her world was falling apart around her. Sleep wasn't coming easily to her and she could tell by the position of the moon that it would be morning in a while. She rolled over, knocking into Willow once more, and the small dragon gave up the fight and crawled off the bed, finding a much more suitable, less interrupted place to rest.

She stared up at the ceiling, tracing every groove in the mud walls with her eyes, reliving her encounters of the day; her experiences in town, when she talked with Neisa, listening to Blaen, and then the warnings of her parents when they returned home earlier that night. It was more than she could wrap her thoughts around, let alone make sense of. Her parents' look of worry said it all.

"Arien, you heard the man. They mean to come after us all if they don't find him," her mother had said as she paced the floor. Ennon and Faineth were still at the table, Faineth's head was still in her brother's lap.

"I know exactly what they said, woman," her father shouted back. "I'm thinking as fast as I can. This is just so much to take in. If the rumors are true and Saigrin really did try and change him, then the question is...why hasn't he returned home?"

"Saigrin?" Faineth questioned her father, lifting her head off of Ennon's lap and sitting up. "Why would you think Saigrin did the changing, Father? He doesn't know how to do that any better than Willow could eat with a spoon. She could try but she

39

would fail, just as I'm sure Saigrin would if he tried performing the changing spells."

"Faineth, how do you know this?" her mother questioned her.

"Everyone knows he can't do it, Mother. He failed every test with the dragon's blood part of the spell. Kept taking from the wrong species and adding it too fast. Lord Melian said he was going to try and show him after courses, so that he could focus better, you know, have more one on one time with him to see where he was messing up. He even asked if I could help, but we hadn't done that yet. Saigrin's a fool if he tried to do the spell, Father."

Faineth's father walked over to the table and sat down next to her. He put his elbows up on the table and rested his head in his hands, rubbing at his temples as if they were about to explode. Her mother walked up behind him and lovingly rubbed his shoulders, in a caressing sort of way, obviously trying to calm him down.

"Arien, don't jump to any ideas before we know everything. It was hearsay, that business about Saigrin, it might not be true," she spoke softly, but her words were not convincing enough that even she believed what she was saying.

"Aye, it's true. He's gone missing as well as this Belamros fella," he said, looking at his family one by one in the small room. "What we need to do now is figure out a way to stay out of Roanus' path."

A state of shock filled the small hut and all four of them fell silent. Faineth knew the desperation of the matter when her eyes met her fathers and they were already filled with tears spilling down his cheek.

"Do you think something has happened to this man, Father, and that is why he is missing?" asked Ennon

"Aye, son, I do. It's the only thing that makes sense. He broke an important alliance and went to the wrong Guardian to do *his bidding; he has paid the price and now we all have to suffer the consequences for a mistake that should have never taken place."*

"I overheard Saigrin's mother say they needed some supplies that they couldn't afford a few weeks ago. Maybe that's what drove Saigrin to do it," Faineth added.

Her father sighed heavily and wiped his face, looking up at her once more. "Whatever did drive him to the madness of performing a spell he wasn't qualified to do, well, it just may have cost all of us our lives…"

Faineth rolled over onto her other side, remembering the words of her father. There had to be a way around it, she thought to herself while she lay sleepless in her bed. There had to be a way that the King and Roanus would forgive them, maybe some other form of punishment. Her mother and father made it sound as if the King's plans were to completely annihilate not only her fellow clansmen, but all the clans and the dragons, as well.

She tilted her head towards her window and the view summoned her out of bed. Willow lifted her head and watched her walk across the room, then turned it down, tucking it under her wing again. Sleep was obviously more important to the dragon then figuring out what Faineth was up to.

She rested her forearms on the worn wooden sill, looking out at the night sky. It was so beautiful and so frightening at the same time. It was the time of night where the moon had settled and the sun had yet to rise and what little light that shone down was cast from the stars above. Like millions of shiny shards of crystal, they littered the sky in a beautiful pattern. She looked down over her village, seeing the silhouettes of the small huts, dark with slumber and a few leftover smoke trails drifting up from stone chimneys of fires too stubborn to fully die and she couldn't imagine the possibility of never seeing this again. The sadness of the thought welled up inside her and she couldn't keep the tears from coming.

Willow looked back up at her again and sensing her mood, flew up and perched herself on the sill next to her. Faineth looked over at her little ally and the thought of something so amazing being destroyed, was more than she could bear.

"There has to be something, anything we can do to stop this horrible thing, Willow," she said through her tears, hugging Willow softly. The dragon burrowed her chin in the crook of Faineth's neck as if she was hugging her back and Faineth wondered if she knew of the danger ahead. She lifted up and looked at Willow's eyes in question and as if she heard every thought, Willow left her companion's embrace and crawled over to the small box in which Faineth kept all of her important, most cherished belongings. Willow gripped the small box in her teeth and brought it over to where Faineth was sitting, laying it in her lap.

"What's this?" she asked, half smiling as she watched. Willow nudged it closer into her lap, beckoning her to open it.

"Alright…alright, don't get too pushy," she teased, opening it slowly. The box itself had been made by her father, out of knotted Firon wood, and he had presented it to her at her last birthday. It was about the size of loaf of bread and had a beautiful carving on the top. It was the letter F intertwined in dragon wings and it was edged in the knotted symbols of their clan, a beautiful tightly braided vine of the Cypress Vine flower.

Inside was a mixed array of what Faineth liked to call her treasures: interesting rocks she had found on trails, beads her mother had made for her hair to wear during ceremonies that called for a nicer outfit, and she even had a piece of Willow's shell that she had kept after she'd hatched, which was now the color of fresh fallen snow. Willow pushed at her hands again, shaking Faineth out of her little glimpses of times past.

"What, Willow? What is in here that you are so desperate to show me?"

Willow stuck out her long tongue and it caught on the edge of a small, folded piece of parchment. It was one of the few tasks Faineth was required to do or that had been asked of her to accomplish when the time was right. Keeping them here was her way of not losing them. As she unfolded it to see what it said, her heart filled with hope instantly. For this task, the time was right and it might be the answer she was looking for. She had almost forgotten all about a meeting she'd had from one of the Fey a week or so ago. It had actually been a meeting her teacher had set up for her, knowing she would be the perfect person to perform it. It took a little time for her parents to warm up to it, but when her teacher let them know he would be going along, their concern had ended. They trusted him, so they knew she would be safe.

They had left the lands of the Eastern Clan, something Faineth had never done before, so it was a true adventure for her and traveled to the shore of the Northern Sea. It would have been a journey that would have taken days for any other Fey, but since they had the fastest form of transportation at their beck and call, the dragons, it only took Faineth and Melian, her teacher, half of a day's time…

"You're going to love it there, Faineth. The sea is so blue and alive. I often take trips there on our off time," her teacher beamed as they rode along on one of the Plains Wyvern's, a dragon suitable in size for a comfortable trip. "I also think you will get along quite well with this person I'm taking you to meet. She's lovelier than the sea itself."

"She lives by the sea?" Faineth asked, quickly thinking of Neisa.

Melian laughed at her question. "No, dear one, she lives in the sea! She's a mermaid with a very special request and I thought you were the perfect person for the job."

"A mermaid? I've never met a mermaid before. What sort of thing would she want from me?"

43

"You'll see, child, you'll see," answered Melian, smiling widely at his protégé.

As they flew over the vast plains of Ethreal, she wondered what it could be, but loving surprises like she did, she decided not to ask any more questions and just enjoy the view. The winter season was right around the corner so the land was blazing in color, from bright reds and soft muted oranges, mixed together with the darkening greens of the trees. The temperatures had already dropped in the mountains causing the glacial rivers to lower, but they still ran clear as glass. She enjoyed every moment of the view. The Dragon Guardians were thought of as outcasts, or gypsies, and most of the Fey world did not accept them as equals, but more rather a necessity to keep around. They were viewed as dirty, unsociable, and devious. None of which was true and for the few folk who ventured upon them or actually sought them out, found out differently. But it was not enough to change the minds of all Ethreal. For this reason, the Guardians traveled a lot within their sections to stay hidden from the rest of Ethreal and didn't venture out to see the world around them unless it was needed, making this truly a gift for Faineth.

They landed in a field next to the shore and the two of them slid off the side of the dragon. The feel of the prickly grass mixed with sand under her feet was a new sensation that made her smile. She watched as the dragon stood back and became invisible, since they were in a different territory and didn't want to cause any problems. It was a lot easier for her and Melian to go unnoticed, not so much for a very large dragon.

Faineth turned towards the sound of the water crashing up against the sand and couldn't help but run to it. She instantly thought of the Elder Twins, Neisa in particular, and understood where their beauty came from. The Sea was magnificent and magical. It reminded her of the deeper sections of the caves of Niramath, in Mt. Liastreil where the dragons dwelled. If the light hit the walls of the caves just right, it would look as if they glowed with stars. The water appeared much the same in the glow of the sun. She lifted her skirt and touched her toes to the water's edge as the next wave came in. It was bitter cold and it made her giggle.

"Is it always this cold, Lord Melian?" she asked, dipping them in again.

"Yes, child, always," answered an unfamiliar yet soothing voice.

Faineth turned quickly to see who had answered her. There was a grouping of large dark gray and black rocks that seemed to rise out of the sand and stretch out far into the ocean, forming a jetty. At the edge of the water, sitting about half way up the rock wall, was a beautiful woman. Well, at first glance, she was a woman, but after looking more closely, she was actually part fish. She had an iridescent greenish-blue tail that draped gracefully into the water underneath her. Each scale was detailed with silver scrolls, delicately edging each curve. The bottom fin looked like the finest sheer fabric, cut in flowing pieces that danced gracefully with the water's movement.

Her hair was the color of aged gold, with strands of pure white, forming long, flowing waves that reminded Faineth of the waves of the sea crashing against the sand. She had tiny delicate shells interwoven that edged her face, dropping down the entire length of her hair, which ended around mid-fin. It was easily the most hair Faineth had ever seen on a person before.

"Hello," Faineth said shyly.

"Hello," answered the beautiful mermaid. "You must be Faineth. Melian has told me so much about you, except he left out how adorable you are," she teased. Faineth could feel the heat in her cheeks and looked down at the sand. Faineth never gave her appearance much thought, but never thought adorable would be used to ever describe her.

"No reason to blush when someone speaks the truth, young one. Come, sit with me here," she continued, patting the rocks next to her.

45

Faineth looked at Melian who nodded in agreement, then quickly made up a story about collecting things for another course, but she knew it was to leave them to their business. She watched as her teacher hurriedly walked down the beach away from them and then turned back around to her new friend.

"Come, I promise I won't bite," she smiled and Faineth knew instantly why these creatures had the nickname of Siren.

She was breathtaking in the beauty department, but when she smiled, it was bewitching. Her eyes actually looked like the deep sea, dark blue and if she wasn't mistaken, they actually rippled like the waves. She took the first few steps toward her and it felt as if she was in a trance. The Mermaid laughed, pulling her out of the enchantment, allowing her to relax a bit.

"You know my name, but I'm sorry, I do not know yours," Faineth said nervously.

"Oh, where are my manners! I'm so sorry, for some reason I feel as if we have known each other for centuries. Old souls will do that, you know. Forgive me, sweet child. My name is Miren," smiled the mermaid.

"Nice to meet you, Miren," answered Faineth, feeling much more at ease then she had a few moments before.

She climbed up the rocks and took her place beside Miren, straightening out her cloak and anchoring her feet so she wouldn't slip off. Sitting next to her, Faineth noticed something odd about Miren. She was expecting a fishy odor, but Miren didn't smell like she lived in the sea. She smelled like she belonged in the garden, her mother's in particular. Her mother's favorite flower was the honeysuckle vine, so she had seven of them in their small yard. She loved them so much, she would even go to great lengths to dig them up and take them with the clan when they traveled to a new resting place. Olorin had told her when she was very little, that one of the vines had actually belonged to her grandmother and it was honoring her memory by taking good care of it. Miren smelled *like the vines Faineth had grown to love almost as much as her mother.*

"You were expecting sea bass or squid?" Miren asked and Faineth instantly realized she was leaning forward and sniffing. She sat upright and almost slipped off the rocks.

"Oh, no...uh...I'm so sorry, Milady; it's just that...you smell of flowers. I wasn't expecting that. Forgive me."

"No reason to forgive. I take it I'm the first Merfolk you have met," she smiled.

"Yes. I haven't met many people really outside of my clansmen. We don't get much opportunity to." Faineth said shyly. "I have met only a few, actually. I think you make number four."

"I see, well, that's alright. I didn't request that you come and see me because of your being well traveled." Miren giggled.

"Why did you ask for me, Milady?"

"Miren, please call me Miren. Milady sounds so...royal." she laughed. "I may have Royal blood in my veins, but I don't necessarily want to be associated with those pompous..." she stopped herself short of finishing the sentence. "Don't get me wrong, little one, I love my family, but sometimes their views are much different from mine, you see."

"Sorry, Mila--Miren."

Miren laughed out loud, splashing her tail into the air.

"See this? This is what I need you for," she said as she watched her own tail sway back in forth in the water.

"Your tail? Not sure what I can do with your tail," Faineth answered.

"Well, I heard you are the person to come to if I want to get rid of it," Miren stated. Faineth was shocked.

47

"Why would you want to get rid of something so lovely? I don't think I know any tail amputation spells and I'm not going to cut it..." she rambled but Miren's laughter cut her short.

"Amputation? Oh my, no! I don't want to get rid of it that way. I want to be a human, silly," she said playfully.

"HUMAN?" Faineth shouted out, but quickly covered her mouth as if they were in a crowded room and she just gave up a very important secret. She looked around, remembering that it was just the two of them sitting there, realizing she couldn't even see Lord Melian anymore. "But you are so beautiful."

"I would like to still be beautiful, Faineth," Miren giggled, "just in human form. You can do that, right?"

"Well, yes, Milady, sorry...Miren, I can but I'm not sure why you would want to. Here you are special, beautiful, and magical. There, well, what does there really have to offer you?" Faineth asked, sounding almost appalled at the idea. The Guardians were the go-to people if a fairy wanted to cross over to the human realm and even become human if they wanted to, but for the life of Faineth, she could never figure out why they would want to.

"This," Miren said softly and pulled out a picture of a somewhat handsome man in a fancy white suit. "This is my Robert and I love him very dearly, you see. I want to be human to be with him, Faineth."

"I see," Faineth said dryly. She didn't think she would ever get why women, of any species, would give up everything for a man. Complete silliness, if you asked her.

"Do you?" Miren asked. "You seem a little...disappointed in my decision."

"I'm sorry, please forgive me. I'll keep my own opinions to myself." Miren laughed at Faineth's words.

"Well, I guess I don't really need your approval, I just need to know if you can do it for me."

"Yes, yes, I can, it's just..." Faineth said but she wanted to argue, do anything to change her mind. It made her sick to think of her giving up her life as a mermaid for some man in a fancy suit.

"Just what? I probably know what you are going to say. 'He's not worth giving up your magic for, he will ruin your life and he isn't like you'... and so on and so on, I've heard it all before."

"Ya, something like that, I guess. It's just hard to understand, is all."

"Well, I can't go and make you understand, but I can give you some time to think about it. I will need your answer soon, though, as he is about to leave for other lands where he comes from and all of this will be for nothing." Miren said with worry in her tone.

"How much time do I have to think about it?" Faineth asked.

"I have until the next full moon Faineth, after that, he will be gone from me forever. If I don't hear from you before then, I will be forced to seek another's help on this. It's something I do not wish to do, as I'm told you are the best at this sort of spell, but if you will not agree, I will be forced to."

Faineth looked into her eyes and knew she wasn't kidding.

"Okay, I will take some time and think about it. You need to make sure that your family supports you with this," Faineth instructed, but saw Miren squirm a bit at the words. "Miren, your family knows of your plans, right?"

"So to speak. Trust me, by the time I hear back from you, all will be well with my plans, I assure you," she said weakly. Faineth looked at her questioningly, but accepted her word.

She took a small piece of parchment out and scribbled the details of the spell out for Miren.

"There's a few things you need to do to prepare first," she started to say and she noticed Miren's excitement in her face, "this doesn't mean I have accepted yet, but it's a just in case sort of thing. You will need to do these things or it will not work and things could go bad."

"Okay, do these or bad things will happen, got it," she beamed.

"Seriously bad things, Miren, and I need to know you will take this to heart. Last thing we need is for it to go bad and you end up deformed, diseased or worse, dead."

Miren's excitement faded a bit and she looked down at her little list of things Faineth had written out as instructions. There were only three things on the little piece of parchment. She needed to find some Arrowroot and make a tea, drinking it five times a day, get plenty of rest and make sure her heart was pure and free, free of guilt, free of pain, and free of doubt. The last part caught Miren off guard a little, knowing she didn't exactly have her family's blessings with this decision, but she wasn't about to share that with Faineth. Miren knew it would be the one solid thing Faineth was looking for to get out of performing the change and that was something Miren would not accept.

"Thank you, Faineth. I will follow your instructions to the tee and wait patiently for your return," she smiled.

As if he knew the meeting was over, Melian returned with an arm load of treasures he had found to take back with them on the journey home. He looked up at the two sitting on the rocks and saw the seriousness of their expressions.

"Oh, I didn't interrupt anything, I hope," he apologized.

"Not at all, Melian," Miren reassured him, "I see you have found what you came for."

"Yes, indeed! I knew this place wouldn't let me down. Never has, I'm sure it never will.

Are we all ready then, Faineth?"

"Yes, Lord Melian, I am," she said then turned back to Miren. "I promise I will take this matter into great consideration. It was very nice meeting you."

"And you as well, Faineth, you as well," Miren said, leaning in to give Faineth a hug. She jerked back for a split second thinking she was about to get all wet and maybe have a touch of sea slime to add to the filth already covering her cloak, but was surprised to feel the silkiness of Miren's skin and absence of wetness. Miren giggled again.

"Remember, sweet child. You will always have something new to learn in life, even when you think you have learned it all," Miren whispered into her ear. Faineth relaxed and hugged her back, thankful and happy that they had met today, no matter the reason.

"Yes, I guess you are right," Faineth answered as she climbed down to start her journey home with Melian.

5. Transformations

The castle was quiet and the sounds of the King's footsteps echoed throughout the East wing. With each step he took, the sharp pain in his forehead increased. This was the part of being the King he hated the most. It was easier when the subjects he needed to deal with harshly were not family.

He rounded the corner and caught sight of his beautiful wife, Anya, and his pain eased a bit.

"Be careful, my husband. Worry lines like that may stick," she whispered in his thoughts.

One of the many unusual gifts in the Fey world that a man and woman shared was the language of telepathy. The Fey called it Whisper Language and it only happened when the two committed to each other in the laws of marriage, but in rare cases, when two were destined by the Maker to be together, it would happen the minute they fell in love. Carrig and Anya were two such beings. Such a gift was given to a couple so that the two would share the most truthful and intimate relationship.

A warm smile spread across Carrig's face as he approached his beautiful wife, who wrapped her arms around his waist as soon as he was near to her.

"Would you love me any less, my dear?" he questioned in silence as he kissed the tip of her nose. Elves were gifted with ability to speak telepathically to their mates, even if their mates were from a different species. Anyone gazing upon the King and Queen would have only witnessed a tender moment between the two.

"Neither the Heavens above, or the pits of the dark below could ever change my heart, my love," she whispered as she placed her head on his chest. "But it's not my choosing you need to change, is it?"

Carrig pulled out of her embrace and hung his head as he looked at the door he was about to go through.

"Oh, that I wish it was, dear Anya."

Carrig smiled one last time at his wife and pushed open the heavy doors to greet his guests.

"Ah! Brother, I was about to send this Satyr to find you," Roanus grumbled, irritating his brother.

"He has a name, Roanus, and you know it. I will appreciate it if you treat my help with more respect than that. No, I know you are upset, but what more can we do? Everything was resolved last night," or at least he had thought.

"No, brother, you decided last night a plan I still do not agree with and now with everything Miren has come to me with, I think my way is the only way."

"Your way, Roanus, is barbaric! I will not sign an order to abolish an entire race of people, all because you want vengeance for Belamros or protection for Miren," Carrig argued. "Justice will be served and your daughter will have the protection she needs, but not that way."

"Justice! You call yourself a man of justice? Carrig, you have been weakened by your love of the clansmen. It has blinded you!" Roanus' shouts were followed by him slamming his fist hard onto the table beside him.

"I will remind you that as I may be your brother, Roanus, I am also your King! Carry that tone with me again and you will be the one who faces my judgment!"

Roanus glared at his brother the king and stomped off towards the door, stopping just before he lifted his hand to open it. He lowered his head in defeat and his shoulders relaxed.

"She's gone, brother," he said so quietly that Carrig almost didn't hear him.

"What? Who is gone?" Carrig asked, seeing the grief in Roanus' face as he turned back towards him. It caused all the anger he had only seconds ago for his little brother to fade.

"Miren. I went to her this morning and I found this," he said, lifting his hand up to retrieve a folded piece of parchment out of his jacket pocket. "I fear the worst has already happened and I am unable to stop it." Many would question his relationship with Miren due to the fact that they were different, but Miren's mother was a Silkie, a Fey known for its ability to live both on land and sea and when she had become pregnant, they knew that the baby would either be Elvin like her father or Merfolk, taking after her mother. It was a risk they both accepted, but after Miren and her sister, Ula were born, their mother and Roanus had split and their mother, Eire, had taken the girls with her, since both were born mermaids and belonged to the sea. Roanus never saw Eire and Ula again, but he remained in touch with Miren in secret.

Without saying anything, Carrig took the parchment from his brother and carefully opened it.

Father,

By the time you read this, it will already be too late. I'm very sorry it had to be this way, but you wouldn't listen and I couldn't marry who you wanted me to. There are things far more important than alliances to me. I love him, Father, I'm sorry.

Forgive me,

Miren

The king, startled by the letter, looked back towards Roanus.

"Now you see where the motivation of my intentions lays, brother. If the same thing happens to Miren that happened to Belamros, I'm not sure I can take it. Please help me stop the clansmen before any more tragedies occur!"

"I still don't think wiping out an entire clan is the answer. What if it isn't too late and she decides to move to the next one? My advice is to listen to her and find one that can do the transformation successfully. That's where Belamros went wrong. He acted in haste and it quite possibly cost him his life."

"Did you not read it? It is too late! I want these...these disgusting excuses for whatever they are...Travelers and I want them all dead!" Roanus roared, an Anya came through the doors, wearing her own version of worry on her face.

"Please keep your voice down, Roanus! The whole castle will be in an uproar in a matter of moments if you don't. I'm sure this matter can be handled in a more calm fashion," she almost pleaded while glancing back at the door like she expected an audience soon.

"I'm so sorry, Anya, but this matter cannot be cream coated. Miren is gone," he said, softening as he handed her the letter. It wasn't a secret in Ethreal that Roanus had had feelings for his brother's wife before they were married. Many thought the way Roanus talked to Carrig some of the time, like he had more authority, was caused by jealousy of what his brother had, including his crown.

"I see..." Anya answered, handing the letter back to Roanus. "What more is there to do, then?"

"To see each and every one of their heads on posts!" Roanus shouted his last words as he stormed out of the room, leaving the King and Queen staring at each other in worry.

~~~

Faineth packed only the things she would need for the spell and glanced back out her window as she hoisted her pack behind her. The night air was still calm, untouched by the sudden sense of urgency in her room.

"Willow, I will need you to do something for me," she asked quietly. "You need to go and ask Simi to meet me just past the marker at the edge of the training field and please do not get side tracked. We need to be as fast as we can, little one," she instructed. Simi was the dragon her and Melian had rode to see Miren the first time, so she wouldn't have to remember too much on how to get there.

Willow nudged her chin under Faineth's then jumped to the window sill and shot off in the night sky towards the caves where the dragons slept. Faineth knew that the dragon would get there before her, so she didn't delay watching Willow fly as she would have if things weren't so urgent. Faineth's favorite thing about the dragons besides their amazing gentleness was their gift of flight.

She quietly tiptoed down the stairs and managed to make a small snack for later, quietly enough that her family did not wake. She also decided to leave a note on the table so that her parents wouldn't worry when they found her missing. Without saying too much, she let them know she and Willow had gone to visit a friend, which would not cause worry as it was something she often did. Grabbing her shawl off of the rack next to the door, she headed out in the still of the darkness to meet her two travel companions.

Just as she suspected, the two dragons were waiting for her at the edge of the field. Seeing her approach; the Plains Wyvern stretched his wings out in ready for departure. Willow was in awe, as was Faineth, at the size of the mighty dragon, something she would never get used to. One thing the Guardians always felt was gratitude for being the ones that were picked to look after these majestic creatures. Willow tried to copy the natural display by stretching out her wings as well and the sight of it caused Faineth to giggle.

"Soon, Willow, soon, but now we have business to attend. Simi, do you remember the way to the North lands Melian and I traveled the other day?" she asked the dragon while climbing up on his head he had lowered for her. The dragon raised his head high after Faineth was safely on and gave a quick nod before taking off in the direction of the sea. Willow flew alongside, effortlessly.

In flight, Faineth went over her lessons to make sure everything she would need to do to complete the transformation would be fresh in her mind. She had everything in her pack to do it successfully. Luckily, she had all the necessary ingredients, which saved them a lot of time they would have needed to gather them. Without agreeing to the transformation earlier, she had started to gather the supplies anyway, just in case.

The dragon's blood was the easy part, it was the Mithium flower that wasn't so easy to find. Although she only needed four petals, it was one of the rarest flowers in Ethreal and only had three petals per flower. The hard part was that they grew separate from one another. Single flowers were often miles apart and often took days for the gatherer to find enough for the spell. Faineth was lucky and with the help of Willow, had found enough in only two days.

The clouds were growing thicker the closer they came to reaching the ocean waters. Faineth wrapped her shawl tightly around her to keep the chill at bay, sensing the smell of rain coming.

"Great, that will help things along," she said to herself sarcastically.

The winds had picked up a little as well and she hoped that a storm wasn't brewing. She had not performed a transformation alone yet and she didn't want her first attempt to go wrong. After finding Miren, they would have to seek shelter if they were going to be successful.

The dragon let out a bellowing sound and Faineth saw that they were close. Tucking close to the back of the dragon, it folded his wings over the top of her and descended to the beach below. Simi landed right beside the rock jetty that she had first met Miren on a few weeks before and she quickly gathered her things and slid off Simi's back. Once she hit the sand, she ran towards the jetty and climbed to the top. Looking out over the Ocean waves, she started to call out to Miren.

"Miren! It's me, Faineth!" she looked out across the sea but saw nothing. "Miren!"

As she went to shout for the third time, she noticed a movement in the waves, but it was so far out she couldn't tell if it was Miren or not. Staring intently in the direction of the movement, a whale surfaced, probably in pursuit of its morning meal, confirming the movement was not Miren.

"You called, my friend?" a voice behind her said, causing her to almost lose footing on the rocks.

"Miren! You startled me!"

"I'm sorry, I wasn't trying to be quiet, forgive me?" she continued to giggle.

Faineth shook her head to calm her heart. As much as it was probably funny, they really didn't have time for joking around.

"Miren, do you still want me to do the transformation?"

"Yes! Oh, yes! Oh, Bless the Maker I was hoping you would do it," Miren said, fighting back her happiness.

"Okay, we need to find shelter. I can't do it if it starts to rain," Faineth said, looking for the closest cave near to them. Not an easy thing to do in the dark.

"Now? Really?" Miren said hesitating a little.

"Have you changed your mind, Miren?" Faineth's heart almost stopped. If she had indeed changed her mind, she was at a loss of what to do to save her people. She suddenly felt her eyes well up with tears as Miren hesitated to answer her question. Seeing it, Miren quickly shook her head.

"No, no, I have not changed my mind, I just…" her words trailed off. " I haven't completely made peace with my father yet about it.

"I'm sure he will understand in time, but we must hurry," she somewhat pleaded with Miren.

"You don't know my father," Miren sighed.

"Should I know your father?" Faineth was surprised at Miren's hesitation. She thought this was something she wanted no matter what the cost.

"Not unless you know the Royal family, the Baelian's."

"I know them," Faineth said, her voice bearing a slight edge of anger to it.

"Then if you know them and you know of my father, Roanus Baelian, you wouldn't act so shocked at my worry," Miren stated, with a nervous giggle at the end.

"Roanus Baelian is your father?" Faineth was shocked, but in a much better way than she could have anticipated. She knew Miren was of a royal family, she just didn't know it was *that* royal family. Miren nodded and sat farther back onto the rocks, resting her elbow against them to support her body.

"So you've met Daddy," she answered sarcastically.

"Your father is about to order all of my kind and the dragons into extinction! I admit when you first came to me, I did not want to do this, but now, knowing who you are, I see it as the only way that he will forgive what has happened to your uncle."

"Maybe, but it might anger him all the more, too," Miren added, sitting up. A deeper wave of worry washed over her, knowing what was about to happen. She didn't question Faineth about what she had heard about her father. That was the one thing that always seemed to get in the middle of their father-daughter relationship. Miren was well aware of her father's anger and how it could easily lead to madness and it was a tough thing to answer. She knew exactly what Faineth was thinking though. Perform a successful transformation and all would be forgiven, but it went deeper than that. Miren was breaking an alliance that her father had struggled for many moons to join together; the marriage to Raziel, a powerful wizard whose alliance would create protection over the royal family, but also whose mere presence made Miren's insides churn. There was no attraction on either's part, as Raziel had other plans, himself.

"That is something I think necessary to chance if it is still something you want Miren, but I need to know now. Rumor has it your father plans on taking his revenge soon. This is the only thing I can think of to maybe stop him. Please, Miren, tell me now what you have decided," Faineth pleaded.

"Yes, Faineth," she paused and smiled down at her. "I do very much still want to do this, but isn't part of the procedure having the blessing of my father?"

"No, I added that so that you wouldn't have any worries or doubts clouding your thoughts," Faineth said nervously, hoping Miren wouldn't be too angry with her.

Miren let out a laugh and startled Faineth once again.

"Oh, sorry, it's just I've been drinking that awful tea for days now and I was so worried I was doing it all for nothing! I even left my Father a note yesterday morning. I have been keeping low ever since."

Faineth smiled wide and a feeling of hope washed over her. She knew this would be the thing that calmed the brother of the King and save all of the clans and most precious to her, the dragons.

"Let's get started then, shall we?" she smiled. "Is there a cave close by? The rain is coming, I can feel it," she said looking around.

"Yes, right past the bend in the jetty. There are several caves on the other side. The seals use them to get away from predators. Come on, if we hurry we will make it before the tide comes in. It will trap us there, but that would be even better right?" Miren smiled wide as did Faineth.

The two hurried along the jetty's rocks and Faineth quickly discovered it was much easier for Miren. She moved across them much as a snake would the sand. She felt a pain in her heart knowing what she was about to give up. But nothing was worth saving more than her people and the dragons and right now that was her first priority. Finally reaching the bend in the jetty, the two quickly climbed down to where the caves were.

Faineth was thankful that most of them were empty and they slid into one closest to the shore. Miren had assured her that as the others would fill up with water, this one wouldn't but reminded her they would be trapped inside until the tide went back out. Faineth thought that would actually work in their favor. If they were going to be discovered and someone would try and stop them from doing the transformation, by the time they were able to be reached, it would be too late and it would already be completed.

They crawled in as far as they could into the cave, which was pretty far, making Faineth wonder if they were enchanted. It also sloped upward, which is why Miren picked it. This was why the water wouldn't reach them and it was large enough that it would trap enough oxygen as well with them to last before the tide released them again. When they went as far as they could, Faineth used a spell to create light for them.

"Illustras Splenedess," Faineth whispered softly and the cave was filled with soft glittering light.

"Beautiful," whispered Miren back. "Now that's a trick I wish I knew how to do."

"I can teach you as soon as we are done. One thing I can't change is your ability to do magic," she reassured a smiling Miren. "This spell only makes you appear human; your life span and your abilities...that will still be there."

"That's wonderful news," Miren sighed.

Faineth carefully laid out everything she would need and picked up a small wooden bowl in which she would mix the potion. She quickly found the flower petals and began to grind them up with a rock she found on the cave floor. After it was mashed to the right consistency, she reached for the Elm sap and added the amount needed to form a paste. Grabbing the vile of dragon's blood, Faineth realized she had forgotten a very important step. To add the dragon's blood correctly, a Guardian must mix the paste with a dragon's scale. Thankfully, there were two, right outside the cave. She carefully placed the bowl on the cave floor and turned towards the opening of the cave.

"Everything okay, Faineth?" Miren questioned.

"Yes, just need one more thing...almost forgot," she admitted. Faineth crawled down and stood at the opening of the cave where she let out a loud whistle. The rains had begun and the water was already up to her knees, crashing a bit more angrily against the rocks then when she had first arrived but within moments, Willow joined her at the edge of the cave. Reaching under the left wing of her little friend, Faineth plucked a scale from Willow, causing her to grimace.

"I promise to make it up to you when we return home," Faineth winked and Willow followed her back to where Miren sat, waiting for things to begin. Miren stroked Willow's head, relaxing her, thanking her for her sacrifice.

Faineth picked up the bowl again and carefully measured out seven drops of the dragon's blood into the small bowl and slowly stirred it with the scale she had plucked from Willow's breast plate. She started to mumble the incantation that allowed it to combine with the paste from the petals and sap and soon it took on a glowing essence that made Miren look on in wonder.

"Do I have to eat that?" she cautiously asked Faineth.

"No," Faineth giggled, "but you do have to wear it."

As soon as the paste was the right consistency Faineth asked Miren once more if this was truly what she wanted to do. Miren nodded and smiled, giving Faineth the go ahead to start. Faineth gathered a small amount of the paste into her hands and lifted it out of the bowl. The glow of it caused the cave to brighten even more.

"A Syreni Ad Humanam," she chanted as she began to rub the paste on Miren's tail. Faineth was taken back at how smooth Miren's tail really was and she felt a slight pang in her heart thinking this would be the last time she ever saw it. Miren twitched a little in discomfort as soon as it touched her scales and Faineth gave her a look of apology without disrupting the chant. It was slightly gritty, but not enough to make her uncomfortable. It was more like the feeling of fine sand washing over her, but there was a mild burning that accompanied it and that was what she reacted to. As soon as she could, Faineth let her in on what was to come.

"Sorry, Miren, it is going to hurt a little, but soon you will sleep and when you wake, it will be done," she tried to smile, but inside she was as nervous as Miren.

Faineth continued the spell until the paste had been rubbed all over Miren's tail, temples, shoulders, and hands and when the last of the ointment had been applied, the cave was filled with an illuminating glow from the paste and Miren relaxed from the pain and fell into a deep sleep. Faineth eased her down so that she was lying comfortably and sat down next to Willow to wait it out. This was the part that no one could teach, the time it took to finish. Everyone was different and since there was no way of telling, Faineth decided now was as good a time as ever to have some breakfast and sneak in a quick nap herself, so she made her way down to the water's edge, which was now halfway in the cave and washed her hands before retrieving the meal she had packed for her and Willow.

They ate their fill and laid out the clothes she had stolen from her mother, for Miren to wear after she woke, before nodding off in the corner. Knowing that she had never had the need for clothing, she didn't expect she would have thought about that part and Faineth knew the particular dress she had taken from her mother's wardrobe, had been one she hadn't seen on her in many moons, so it wouldn't be missed.

It seemed as if hours had passed and Faineth still couldn't relax enough to find some sleep herself. She stared at Miren wondering if it was working or if she had messed up something when mixing the paste and had in turn killed her. She must have gone through the formula a hundred times when her body froze at the thought of what would happen if she had hurt Miren. She knew there would be nothing to stop Roanus then.

Willow laid her head in Faineth's lap as if she felt the worry, too. It wasn't just Faineth's people that were under threat; it was Willow's, as well. The two snuggled close together in worry just as the paste on Miren started to fade. Willow's head lifted and she let out a small cry.

"I really hope for our sakes she makes it, little one," Faineth said softly to Willow but not taking her eyes off of Miren. The little dragon let out a small moan and dropped her head in Faineth's lap as if in agreement.

6. Blood Lust

The King paced across the floor as Anya sat in the chair, looking worriedly at her husband.

"Do you have any ideas, my love, other than the ones of pure hatred your brother is offering?" she asked. He stopped at the far side of the room and turned around, slowly looking back at her as if she brought him out of a trance.

"I'm sorry, forgive me, I didn't hear you. What was it you said?" he responded, stress clearly written all over his face.

"Isn't there anything else we can do? Do you really believe that the destruction your brother is speaking of is really the answer? There has to be another way. Please tell me you think he is mad, Carrig, and that you are not in agreement with him," she pleaded.

"By the blood of our son, I am not in agreement with him over this!" he shouted but calmed a bit, seeing the fear in his wife's eyes. He quickly walked over to her, dropping to his knees, and laid his head in her lap. "What I fear most is that the people will side with him over this. You know how they view the Guardians. They don't even refer to them by their right names…Travelers or whatever, any way you look at it, it's not looking good. If I do what's right, we could face a problem much greater than losing them."

"What's greater than completely destroying an entire race of two living things? What madness has come to make you truly believe that? I would rather face people knowing that we had done the right thing than listening to them applaud us with so much

65

blood on our hands!" Anya couldn't fight her tears any longer and struggled free of her husband, running out of the room. The King laid his head back down in the empty chair and began to weep himself.

~*~

Roanus entered the room and closed the door behind him. He turned around towards the three men standing before him and motioned them to gather closer to his side. The room was dark and filled with an eeriness you could cut with a knife. Even the light of the fire that was almost out in the massive fireplace gave little warmth.

"I will have the King's approval of this before the rise of the sun. We will set out within the hour to attack the caves. Once you have destroyed the dragons, you will head to the villages and destroy everything in your path. We will not be taking prisoners, so keeping any of the filth alive is not an option. Anyone caught hiding or aiding these…creatures…will be executed without trial. Do I make myself clear, gentlemen?" Roanus, seeing the unease of his men, made sure they did.

"I have men already on their way to the other clans with the same orders. When you are finished, I want you all to report back to me," he continued.

"And you are sure the King has approved this, Roanus?" questioned Peadar, the King's commanding officer to his personal guard.

Roanus closed the gap between him and Peadar, standing just inches away from him.

"Do you actually think I would go behind the back of my own brother, my King, Peadar? Do you really think me so ignorant?" he said in a threatening tone. The rest of the men in the room fidgeted slightly in discomfort of what they were seeing.

None of them thought this was in fact orders of the King, but none of them ever wanted to cross Roanus, either.

"No, my Lord, forgive me," Peadar answered, standing straighter to define allegiance, but secretively thought of ways to get word to the King before his men carried out the order, just to be on the safe side.

"And, if any of you think of disturbing my Brother tonight to challenge what I have said, you will be wasting time and offending his order...and you will displease me greatly, as well. I'm the hand of the King now and not for folly," he added as if he could sense exactly what Peadar was thinking.

"Yes, my Lord," the men answered in unison and quickly left the room. Roanus crossed it and sat down in the chair next to the fireplace. The fire was warm and helped him relax a little.

"Vengeance will be mine and not even you, Brother, can stop me," he confessed into the flames. "And when all this is done, I'll have your kingdom, as well."

~*~

The king wiped his tears, knowing that this would not solve any problems that he must now face. Peadar had betrayed Roanus and shared his plans with the king, but it had been too late for them to change anything. He crossed the room and opened the door, requesting the guard that was standing right outside to send for his son, Faolan. He closed the door and paced the floor, waiting for Faolan's arrival. He had an idea. It wasn't an idea to solve everything in this nightmare his brother was creating, but it would at least help and save some of the people he and his family had grown to love. Within minutes, Faolan was standing in the doorway.

"Father?" Faolan questioned, startling the King.

"Ah, Son, yes, close the door, will you?" Carrig said softly. "This is for no other's ears but yours. There is something we need to do and it needs to be done with great speed and as inconspicuously as possible."

"Anything, Father, just name it and it is done," Faolan reassured his father, closing the gap between them.

"I was hoping that you would say that, Son," Carrig answered, wrapping his arm around his son's shoulder, turning the two of them towards the blazing fire and started to quietly unveil his plan.

7. Annihilation

The sounds of the waves crashing, as well as the gulls fighting over what the tide had left them to eat as it journeyed its way back to the sea, stirred Faineth out of her sound sleep. She looked down and smiled at the sight of Willow sleeping peacefully in her lap. She reached her hand up and stroked her soft, scaly head and laid her head back against the rock. The sun was up as she could see the light coming through the entrance of the cave. Faineth suddenly remembered where she was and what she was doing there.

She sat straight up, causing Willow to awaken as well and the dragon crawled over to a quieter spot, obviously not ready for the day to begin. She looked around the cave as her eyes adjusted, but there was no sight of Miren anywhere. Immediate panic set in and Faineth jumped up, searching the cave more extensively. Miren would need help with her new legs and Faineth was worried that if she tried to crawl, or worse, walk off alone, she would end up hurting herself.

Frantically, she stumbled out of the cave, looking up and down the beach for any sign of Miren. The sun was out in full glory, making the rocks and sand warm. She climbed back up onto the jetty to get a better look and when she reached the top, she couldn't help but smile wide at the sight of Miren. She was beautiful, even more so Faineth thought, now that she had legs. She was walking along the water's edge, letting the waves crash onto her feet, giggling and kicking at the water, enjoying the new feelings. The morning's sunlight danced on her hair that swayed gently in the breeze and threatened to touch the water. Her mother's dress appeared as if it was a little big, but Faineth thought that was better than if it had been too small. She smiled as she noticed Miren touching the softness of the fabric and grabbing it, twirling it around her new legs as she walked.

"I'll take that as a sign you like the new you, then?" Faineth called out to her.

"Faineth! Look at me! I'm walking, I'm really walking, and I'm dancing," she continued as she began to twirl around in the water. Faineth giggled and climbed off the rocks to meet her.

"I'm quite impressed, actually," Faineth beamed. "Usually it takes a lot longer for those to work like that," she said pointing down at Miren's new legs.

"They're really something! I think I came to sometime in the middle of the night and it looked as if you and Willow had just fallen asleep and I didn't want to disturb you. I've been practicing for a while now," she blushed.

"Maybe so, but I've seen it take days, so I'm still going to brag about you," Faineth smiled and grabbed Miren's hands and the two twirled around at the water's edge together, laughing as if there wasn't any threat lurking in the background of their future.

Faineth would remember this day for as long as she was alive, she knew that much. They stopped briefly to catch their breath. The sun that was reflecting off the ocean was warm on Faineth's back. Miren was looking at it over Faineth's shoulders and the way the sun's sparkling reflection danced in Miren's eyes, took her breath away. It reminded Faineth again of the Caves of Niramath, where the walls sparkled like they were painted with pixie dust.

Without warning, Miren's expression changed and her eyes grew dark. Faineth reactively frowned with her.

"Faineth," Miren mumbled, "look."

Faineth turned around and looked out over the waters to see what had startled Miren. There, in the middle of her view, sat three large ships, but that wasn't what truly caught her eye. All around the ships and mostly in the middle of them, the water was crashing about as if a storm had dropped down in the middle of them without warning or disturbing the surrounding waters, except the sky was clear of any clouds. Some of the waves were actually taller than the ships themselves causing Faineth to gasp.

"Oh, Miren! They will sink for sure!" Faineth cried out.

"No, Faineth, the ships are what's causing the troubled waters," she choked out then gasped and clapped her hands over her eyes. "No...NO!"

"Miren? What is it? All I can see are ships and waves! What's happening?" she demanded.

Faineth knew that some Fey had the ability to see clearly for miles. Miren was obviously one of them and she apparently didn't lose this ability in the transformation.

"It's so awful!" Miren replied.

"Miren! I can't see it like you can! Please, tell me what is happening!" Faineth urged.

"They're killing them!" she shouted back and then her knees buckled, causing Miren to sink down onto the sand.

A loud bellowing sound came from behind them on the shore and Faineth looked away from the crumpled heap Miren had become to see Simi. To her, it looked as if he was crying right along with Miren. She instinctively looked around for Willow, but there was no sign of her. She wondered if she was still in the cave sleeping. She looked back at Simi who was now standing straight up on his hind legs, as if he was trying to see everything that was happening in the water.

"Miren, who is killing who?" Faineth asked, grabbing her friend by the shoulders. "You have to tell me!"

"The dragons…Sena…and Neisa! They're killing them and it's all entirely my fault!"

Faineth turned sharply in the direction of the water and froze and the tears fell down her cheeks effortlessly from her wide eyes. She felt as if she was about to faint and probably would have if Simi hadn't let out another large bellow followed by flames, shooting from his mouth, high into the sky.

"It's begun, Faineth, you have to go and warn your people! This has my father written all over it, but there still might be time!" Miren pleaded. "Go, Faineth…now!"

Faineth caught her breath and wiped her eyes with the ends of her shawl. A movement on the rocks caught her attention and when she looked over, she saw Willow staring out to the sea. The small dragon looked as horrified and as angry as Simi did.

"Will you be okay?" she asked Miren as soon as she found her voice again.

"Faineth, I will be fine! You need to stop worrying about me and start worrying about you and your people! Go child, you need to hurry!" she yelled through her own tears.

Faineth threw her arms around Miren in a goodbye embrace, as if it was going to be the last time the two would see each other.

"I hope to see you again someday, Miren," she whispered with false hope.

"If we make it out of this alive, you can count on it, my dearest Faineth," she answered back, sounding just as bleak and kissed her cheek softly.

Without looking back, Faineth ran towards Simi and quickly climbed onto the back of the dragon, giving the signal to head home. The large Dragon looked out across the ocean one last time, let out a large cry, spread its wings, and shot into the air, almost knocking Faineth off in the process. Her shawl, that she had thrown around her shoulders loosely, flew off and drifted back down to the beach. Faineth looked back in the direction of her wrap, but didn't think twice of its loss. She was numb, so the chill of the storm didn't affect her. Not till later, when she knew her people, most of all her family, were safe, would she feel the loss of the warm gift her mother had made for her.

She was sick with fear as she made the journey, which now seemed unbearably long, to her village. She laid down on Simi, sensing the mighty dragon was feeling many of the same emotions Faineth was, but also because the light headedness had not passed. So many thoughts raced through her mind. Fear and panic were quickly setting in. She worried that they wouldn't make it back in time to warn her people of the dangers that lie ahead and that she would have to see a similar nightmare play out before her again. She thought of Neisa and her heart felt a pain as if it truly had broken apart. A friendship like theirs was rare and Faineth knew it and now it was gone forever.

A soft wail sounded just behind her and she turned to see Willow. The small dragon looked stricken with grief and worry and Faineth sat up and turned towards her. Willow flew in closer to her and she noticed another expression…fear.

"Stay by me, Willow, and I swear on my life, yours will be safe," Faineth shouted out to her.

As if that was all Willow needed to hear, she closed the gap between them and landed on Simi, curling up in front of Faineth. Simi turned her head slightly and saw that the two of them were on her back and begun to pick up speed. Realizing that the dragon had been flying at a speed that Willow could keep up with, Faineth bent down over Willow and grabbed Simi's reigns and bound them tightly around her wrists, ensuring that they were secure on Simi's back. Giving a tap to let Simi know they were ready, the large dragon responded and extended his wings out to full length. With a few large flaps, he was at top speed, making it hard for Faineth to see, so she closed her eyes.

Faineth suddenly heard a loud, strange sound and forced her eyes open to see. The wind that was still beating against her face caused her eyes to water, making it hard to really focus on the terrain below her. A dark mass moved along the land under them and she strained to see what it was. Simi did as well and then instinctively, the dragon lifted them higher into the sky. Faineth then realized what the mass was. Several men, Fey to be exact, lined up as soldiers would for battle, moving slowly toward her village.

"Simi!" Faineth shouted, "Faster, Simi, faster!"

The large dragon turned towards Faineth then looked at the swarm below. As if Faineth herself gave Simi the orders, he lowered his head and plummeted towards the army below, showering the ground below them with fire. The heat from the flames rose and pricked at Faineth's skin and she tucked her and Willow in closer to Simi's back. Willow unfolded her wings and wrapped them around Faineth as if she was hugging her, but what she was doing was protecting her. Dragon's scales were unique in the fact that not only did they not burn; they also did not feel heat and she was instantly cooled off.

Faineth heard as the men cried out in pain and instantly hoped that the one Elf she knew and loved was not there and at the same time, hoped that Simi had destroyed them all. She tried to tell herself that her friend would not partake in an act so cruel and that seemed to comfort her a bit, but what rose deep inside Faineth now was bigger than fear, she was angry. She had never felt that way before and it was shocking to her.

"Again, Simi!" she shouted out and the dragon circled back around, sinking lower into the sky to hover just above the men bellow and released another large flame, covering the ground under them, engulfing everything in its path.

More screams of pain and death cried out into the night sky and it was more than Faineth could take. Lifting her hands as much as the reigns would allow, she covered her ears as Simi made a third pass at the ground below. Faineth nudged her side to let him know that was enough and the dragon lifted back into the air, finishing the journey home. Faineth hoped that that would at least buy her clan some time.

Simi let out another bellow and Faineth opened her eyes again to see the outline of her village, a strange orange glow along the horizon's edge. Smoke arose from the roof tops and dragons of many different species were flying wildly in the air above. Horror grew in her heart knowing she was too late.

8. Heartache

Ennon woke to the sounds of his parents clashing about in the hut bellow. His mind was still a bit groggy from the late night before, but he managed to get dressed and climb down the rickety make shift stairs without falling.

"Ennon, good, you're awake. Go wake Faineth. We haven't much time," Olorin ordered her son, as she quickly shoved things from all corners of their hut into her skirts to fill the few sacks she had laid on their small table.

Ennon looked around and noticed his father was in as much hurry as his mother, packing food items into a larger sack used mainly for seeding. He glanced over out the window, as movement outside caught his attention. Many of the clansmen appeared to be in the same kind of frenzy.

"Ennon!" shouted his father. "You heard your mother, lad. Go wake Faineth. We are leaving here soon. She will need time to gather her things as well and when you are finished getting her up, go to your room and pack anything you can't live without for the next few months without getting too carried away. We need to pack as light as we can for travel. Please do me the favor and let your sister know the same, will ya?"

Arien spoke so quickly, Ennon almost missed half of what he said.

"We have no time for you to wrap your head around it, Son! Go!" Arien shouted again at his son.

Ennon stumbled back up the stairs and went down the small hall to where Faineth's room was. He poked his head inside the door, looking in the direction of her bed, but noticed right away that it was empty. He ran inside, looking around the tiny room and then out the window. He turned back around and saw that Faineth had left a small note on her table. Quickly opening it, Ennon read as fast as he could then called out to his parents as he made his way back down the stairs.

"Pa! She's not here! Look!" he shouted, practically throwing the note in his father's direction. Arien looked it over and his hands dropped to his sides. Faineth's parents knew about Miren's request, but thought Faineth was against it, so they had not worried about it again, until now.

Olorin stared at her husband in fear, "What, Arien? What is it? Where's Faineth?"

"She's gone and done the changing and knowing her, it will be already done," Arien said in a defeated tone.

Olorin sunk to her knees, spilling the contents of her skirts out onto the floor. Ennon crossed the room to comfort his mother, when a sound came from the door. The three of them looked into each other's eyes as if it would be the last time they could. The banging at the door grew louder and Arien stiffened with fear.

"By the Maker's grace, I shall see ya again," he whispered to his wife, whose tears were now flowing steadily down her cheeks.

"I love ya both," Olorin started to say her goodbye to her family but was cut short when the door gave way crashing open.

~*~

Simi landed at the edge of the village, around the backside of the training fields as it seemed to be the safest place at the moment. Faineth quickly got her and Willow down and the minute her feet touched the ground, Simi gave her a nod and was back in the air. The movement almost caused Faineth to almost fall, but she managed to stay upright. She quickly ran over to some brush and ducked down, crawling underneath to try and get as close to her hut as possible. She had to see for herself if her family was okay. The air was thick with smoke and heat, making it hard to see at first, but her eyes adjusted after a while, letting her fully comprehend the damage before her. Where her village once stood vibrant and full of life, was replaced with complete and consuming destruction. Through the flames and smoke, she could see the ruined outlines of what used to be her clans people's homes. Most of them had been burned to the ground or torn apart by something larger than Faineth couldn't even begin to understand. She knew evil existed, but was never aware it could exist on this level.

"Willow, this is where you go warn the other dragons. Please don't worry about me. I'll find you, as soon as I know my family is okay," she said, hugging her little friend, hoping that Willow wouldn't see through her lie. Faineth was beyond scared, but the one thing she could not face was watching Willow destroyed and if there were men still here, she would protect her at all costs, including sending her away.

Willow nodded at her then turned and flew over to where the caves were, leaving Faineth to hope there were some dragons still inside seeking shelter. It was a bleak idea, seeing most of them in the sky, doing their best to stay alive. The hissing sound of arrows and whispering sound of magic filled the air, causing her to cup her hands over her ears. Most of the battle was beyond her; as if they had done what they could here and moved on. Only a few still lurked in the shadows, but Faineth was small enough, she knew she could move about undetected. The heat of the still burning fires seared at her skin, but she didn't seem to notice. She was completely focused on staying alive and finding her family.

Thankfully, Faineth knew the layout of the village well and could easily get around without having to see too much. The smell of death was starting to overwhelm her senses, causing her stomach to sour and she leaned against what used to be the store house where the clan stored the dried meats for the winter. Luckily, the hunting season for the winter months had just begun so it wasn't at its fullest. Smelling the burning meat and knowing there was nothing she could do about it forced her to keep going and it made her think of Miren again. Her heart hurt thinking that she, too, was in danger. If her father was really this evil, what was in store for Miren when she returned to Castle Baelian? Faineth shook her head at the thought, hoping her friend wouldn't even consider the idea of going there.

She finally made it to the edge of the huts and where the chaos had died down, in its stillness, she noticed the degree of death that surrounded her. Standing up, without thinking, Faineth finally took a good look around. Bodies laid strewn out haphazardly across the ground, some in heaps as if their last effort was to protect the one who was underneath them, some damaged beyond recognition. Smoke rose from huts and carts that used to be filled with straw and supplies and the body of one of the Wyvern's, she recognized as Tala, a training dragon, laid across the rooftop of Master Melian's hut and Faineth ran towards it without thinking.

"Lord Melian?" she cried out in horror, hoping for the sound of her teacher, but nothing came. She approached Tala carefully, but noticed it was too late for the dragon. Pools of her blood lay around her body, mixing with the dirt of the ground. As she followed it out, the blood changed color to a darker red and that's when she saw her once loved teacher, face down and still. She went to him and when she reached him, another hope vanished. Melian's throat was cut and his still open eyes showed no sign of life. Faineth reached down and closed his eyes with her fingers, saying a quiet prayer for his soul's peace, as tears stung her cheeks. She got up and continued on her path towards her family's home.

She glanced over to her left and noticed a pile of hay with a body laid across the top. She rubbed her eyes to try and clear them to make sure she was seeing correctly when the person moved again. Someone was alive! She ran towards it, having to jump over yet another dead clansman she recognized as Phaedra, a girl that was a few years older than she was, who used to bug Ennon because of the crush she had on him. Faineth had never really liked her because of it, but seeing her like that, she felt horrible. She pushed her feelings aside and reached the body that had moved only moments before. They were lying face down in the hay, with four arrows piercing them through the back. She gasped at the sight and the sound caused the body to moan. Faineth quickly picked the hay off the person and she gasped again. She would recognize that wild, fuzzy, brown hair anywhere.

"Blaen," she whispered as she slowly turned him over to face her. His face was wrinkled in pain from her turning him, but when he opened his eyes and saw her face, he smiled.

"Ah, I knew you'd find me sooner or later," he said, but winced again in pain. His voice was familiar yet there was something off and his breath gargled when he breathed and Faineth knew that some of the arrows had pierced his lungs.

"Blaen…I…" she tried to speak but it was like the words were stuck in her throat. She wanted to drop her face and cry, but she couldn't take her eyes off of him.

"Aye, I've really gotten myself in a grand mess this time," he coughed on the last word and moaned in pain. Seeing the look on her face when he opened his eyes caused him to frown a bit.

"Ah, but it's not much pain," he lied, "I should be better in a few minutes."

She giggled nervously at his attempt to make things look better than they were, but tears continued to stream down his face.

"That bad, aye?" Blaen laid his head back against the hay, but kept looking at Faineth who only nodded to answer his question. "Ah, well, that wasn't what I had in mind when today started," he winced again, but she could see how painful even talking was for him, so she edged closer and lifted his head to rest in her lap.

"Shh, Blaen. I'll stay with ya…till it's time," she said trying to calm, but the last words came out sounding more like she was being choked. There was a lump in her throat the size of a stone and she fought back the huge sob that was trying to escape. She didn't want the last thing he would hear alive to be her crying. She let her head lean back a bit and she started to hum a tune of one of the songs she knew he loved as a small child and mindlessly rubbed his hair as he watched her.

> *"Sleep, O babe, for the red-bee hum, the silent twilight's fall:*
> *Aibheall from the Grey Rock comes to wrap the world in thrall.*
> *A leanbhan O, my child, my joy, my love and heart's-desire,*
> *the crickets sing you lullaby. Beside the dying fire,*
> *Dusk is drawn, and the Green Man's Thorn is wreathed in rings of fog:*
> *Siabhra sails his boat till morn upon the Starry Bog.*
> *A leanbhan O, the pale half-moon hath brimmed her cusp in dew,*
> *and weeps to hear the sad sleep-tune I sing, O love, to you."*

He moved a bit and settled deeper in to her lap and she knew his last breaths were coming, so she skipped to the last verses and watched his face as she continued.

> *"Faintly sweet doth the chapel bell ring o'er the valley dim:*
> *Tearmann's peasant-voices swell in fragrant evening hymn.*

A leanbhan O, the low bell rings my little lamb to rest and angel-dreams,

till morning sings its music in your head.

Sleep, O babe, for the red-bee hums the silent twilight's fall,

Áibheall from the Grey Rock comes to wrap the world in thrall.

A leanbhan O, my child, my joy, my love and heart's-desire,

the crickets sing you lullaby beside the dying fire,"

Her voice wavered on the last part of the song as Blaen took his last breath, relaxing completely into her lap, with a peaceful smile on his face. At least she would always take comfort in the fact that she could give him that before he died. She laid his head back down in the hay and after closing his eyes, she softly kissed his cheek.

"May the road rise up to meet you," she whispered in his ear and stood up and walked away without looking back. She reached the center of the village before the gruesome reality of what used to be her home was too much and Faineth dropped to her knees, finally emptying her stomach on the ground.

9. Deliverance

After a few minutes, a movement in front of her shook her back into full consciousness and she quickly got back onto her feet, running behind a hut that was next to her parents'. She relaxed a little when she saw what caused the movement. A small cat had run across the way into the woods to probably seek shelter. She took a deep breath and cleared her head. She had to see for herself if they had suffered the same fate as the rest of the village, no matter how horrific it might be to see. She would never be able to live with herself if she assumed they were dead when they weren't. It was worth the risk of her safety to find out.

She made it to the backside of her family's hut without being noticed and quickly climbed through one of the back windows. It was quiet inside and her first instinct was to call out for her family, but decided against it. She looked in the two rooms' downstairs, opening larger cupboards or anything big enough they could have hidden in and found nothing. She went upstairs to where they slept and found more emptiness. The strangest part was that there was no sign of struggle; nothing turned upside down, nothing broken, nothing torn; just emptiness, as if they had packed almost everything and just walked out the front door.

Faincth stood in the middle of the kitchen and stared at the bareness of her family's hut. "Where could they be?" she wondered out loud, as she mindlessly looked around. Had they seen her note and gone to look for her? Her heart leaped a little at the idea. If they did do that then maybe they were safe somewhere, but how would she find them? Would they run into trouble along the way? The thoughts flooded her mind as she continued to look around, causing her not to hear the sound of footsteps behind her.

"Faineth," he whispered and sent the girl into full blown panic.

She jumped nearly out of her skin and scurried into the corner behind the kitchen table.

"Who are you and what do you want? Please don't kill me, the change was a success!" she shouted out to the intruder.

"Faineth, why on my Father's crown, would I ever want you dead?"

She instantly recognized the voice of her visitor and relaxed a bit. Standing up, she adjusted her eyes to see, taking in the elf that stood in her mother's kitchen.

"Faolan?" she asked, still on the cautious side.

"Come out from behind the table, please, Faineth. I'm here to help you, silly girl, not to harm you," he said softly. She ran forward, almost leaping into his arms and he rubbed her head softly trying to calm her. "I already delivered your family to the safe house; I've only come back for you and that white dragon of yours," he added.

White dragon…

"Willow! Oh no, she went to the caves! Faolan we have to go get her!" Faineth cried out, burying her face in his cloak.

The elf stood at least three stones higher than Faineth and had wings that were taller than he was, but he never made her feel small. Faolan was a longtime friend of her family and son of the King, Carrig Baelian. The families had spent a lot of time together when Faineth was little, but as of late and with three moves in the last ten years for Faineth's family, time together was rare.

"I'm sure Willow is just fine. I've never met a more brave and cunning dragon, Faineth. Besides, she is your shadow. She will sense that you have left and follow, I'm sure of it. Now, we need to get you out of here before the men find us. My father sent me, but his brother, my uncle, won't take heart to my being here." Faolan wiped her face and handed her a cloak.

"What's this?" she asked, calming down a bit. Knowing that her family was safe made it easier to deal with her surroundings.

"This, my friend, is what is going to get you out of here. It's of Elvin magic. The perfect disguise for all who want to slip away from danger," he joked.

"Am I supposed to wear this?" Faineth tugged at the material of the wrap, pulling at it as if it were miles long.

"Well, yes, I wasn't expecting you to eat it. No worries, you'll be on my back. The material has been spelled, so there won't be any way possible for any of the men out there to see you with it on.

"If you are sure…" she said, halfheartedly as she wrapped the oversized cloak around her shoulders and fastened the clasp on the front under her chin.

"Faolan," she whispered, "are my parents okay? Is Ennon okay?" she choked out, tears streaming down her face.

"Yes and they are very anxious to see you, so let's not keep them waiting any longer, alright?"

Faineth nodded and climbed up on the chair, making the hoist up on Faolan's back an easier task.

"We are going to do this…uh… my way, okay? It's faster." Faolan said in a sheepish tone. "Trust me."

"Always." Faineth said, but before she fully understood the meaning of his request, Faolan's body began to quiver and shake, making noises Faineth associated with the breaking of bones.

"Faolan!" she called out.

"Stand back little one. Sometimes this gets a little…" he tried to finish but fell to the ground instead. His back arched and Faolan let out what sounded like a whimper, then a deeper guttural noise. His wings coiled back onto themselves and seemed to disappear into his back. Within seconds, Faolan's skin was darkening, with hair growing from every pore.

"Faolan!" Faineth shouted and jumped off the chair; retreating once again to the corner behind the table. From the angle she was standing, she couldn't see him fully anymore, but was glad of it.

"…messy," he said, finishing his sentence and Faineth gasped when he stood up again, only this time he was standing on all fours.

"Faolan...you're a...you're a...what are you?" she choked out in shock.

"Canidae Lupis Major is what the scholars have called me, but people in the human world refer to me as a wolf," he said, half proud and half embarrassed. "It was a little something passed down from my mother's side of the family."

"A...wolf, as in a Werewolf?"

Faolan nodded his head in answer.

"Not sure I've ever seen just a...wolf...before," Faineth said, using caution on the word 'wolf' as to not mess it up.

"And you wouldn't have, as there are no wolves in Ethreal. Just me...strange, huh?" he said, turning his head around to look her in the eyes.

Faineth slowly came out from around the table. Faolan, in his wolf form, stood a little taller than Faineth. His fur was as dark as his Elvin hair, but much thicker. She ran her hand along his back and it felt soft on her skin. She walked around him and settled on his face. It was his eyes that Faineth recognized immediately. She would have known it was him because of those eyes. They were exactly the same. Deep, stormy, brooding eyes.

"Not weird." Faineth said pausing and then a smile spread hugely across her face. He breathed a sigh of relief and it caused her hair to fluff up around her face. "You are the most amazing thing I have ever seen!" she giggled.

"You guard and ride on dragons and I'm the most amazing thing you have seen?" Faolan questioned her, half laughing. "You really must get out more, then," he teased, moving closer to her so she could climb on his back.

"Are you sure it won't hurt?" she asked.

"What, you riding on my back? I'll be more surprised if I feel you at all up there. Now, come on, we don't have any time to waste. I can hear better in this form and it sounds like another surge is coming."

Faineth didn't wait around for instructions on how to get onto Faolan's back. She hoisted herself up on the chair and practically jumped over onto him.

"Make sure every inch of you is covered by the cloak; we don't want any fingers or toes sticking out."

Faineth looked around and after seeing that she was well covered, she pulled it over her head, concealing herself completely. He wasted no time after Faineth was hidden and turned, heading out the same way he came in. He was large, but because of his darker color and his ability to move with almost no sound, Faolan was confident that they would make it out of there safely.

10. Loss

Knowing her family was safe and she was to reunite with them soon, Faineth let the stress and heartache of the night go and she fell deeply asleep on Faolan's furry back. It was surprisingly a smooth ride, but with everything that had been happening, she didn't seem to think it odd. In fact, she was becoming numb. She was caught somewhere in between panic and exhaustion.

Dreams came but nothing made sense. It wasn't realistic, but it was disturbing. Clouds of darkness billowed around her like that of a bad storm at sea. There was nothing around her except for glimpses of dragons in turmoil, caught in the wind like puppets, unable to control their movements. Faineth reached for them without any success of actually touching them. All she could do was watch. Brightness flooded her view and she placed her hands over her face, but instead of the feeling of fingers, her hands felt like soft wisps of ribbon, tickling at her skin.

Rolling over and waking up slightly, she realized quickly that the ribbons were actually her own hair, moving across her face in the morning breeze and the light was the sun slowly rising on the horizon. She looked around a little more and suddenly realized she was no longer on the back of a wolf, but lying, alone, in a patch of soft heather.

"Faolan!" she rose up, calling out and the panic and memories of the night before rushed back to her.

"I'm here, Faineth," Faolan answered off in the distance. He was back in his Elvin form, carrying something in the hem of his shirt.

"I'm sorry, I should have wakened you, but you looked as if you could really use the sleep. Besides, I couldn't let our last bit of the journey go on empty stomachs." Faolan giggled, loosening his shirt and letting his bounty fall to the ground. Several apples rolled out onto the ground and a few made it to Faineth, one bumping her in the foot. She quickly reached for it, not waiting for permission to take the first bite. It was juicy and delicious and didn't take long for Faineth to finish before she was reaching for her second.

"Ah, you were hungry," Faolan teased, as if there were nothing wrong in their world. That was one of the many things she loved about the Baelian's, well most of them, anyway (Faolan and his parents, to be exact). No matter what was happening around them, good or bad, they always were the most caring, compassionate, and fun people.

"You could say that," she mustered to say through the bits of apple sloshing around in her mouth. "How much farther do we need to travel before we come to the safe house?"

"Not much farther. It's just over those hills there," he said pointing out to a grouping of large mounds of earth.

She looked around a little more and realized she had never been here before. The ground was covered in soft hues of pink, white, and green. The colors were muted as if they were in a fog, yet the air was clear. It was relatively flat, but after looking some more, it actually sloped out away from them, as if they were sitting inside of a large bowl.

"Where are we, anyway?"

"We, my little one, are in the Valley of the Mist. Eidolon Forest is just beyond those boulders behind you.

Faineth turned sharply, staring back at what they had journeyed through.

"You brought us through Eidolon Forest?" she gulped, "And we made it out of there...alive?"

Faolan laughed at her worry. "Well, considering that we must have looked just as scary as some of the things said to inhabit the forest, I would have to say, that it was as safe a journey as anyone could hope for. No need to worry Faineth, we won't be going back that way," he smiled.

Faineth relaxed her shoulders and her body let loose a shiver at the same time. The stories she had been told about Eidolon Forest and the Valley of the Mist would conjure the deepest nightmares in anyone. She shivered again and turned to look at Faolan.

"And I suppose you are immune to all that stuff?" she asked him in awe.

"No, not necessarily, just focused, I guess you could say. I wasn't going to let a few scary folklores determine your safety. Speaking of which, are you about done massacring those apples?"

"Yes, of course I am," she said as she scooped up the remaining apples and stuffed them under the hem of her jacket. Faolan laughed at the sight of her. "What?" she blushed, half embarrassed, half annoyed.

"Nothing," he answered, still smiling as he reached for a bag Faineth hadn't noticed before. He folded the cloak she had worn the night before and neatly tucked it inside. Faineth chuckled as she saw that it barely made a lump in the deep red velvet bag.

"Will I ever learn all there is to know about you…this place…everything?" she said, holding her arms out as if to point everywhere at the same time.

"Well, now there is a question. Considering, I'm three times your age and I still have many, many things to learn, I would suggest if that is your goal in this life, you'd best get started," and with that, he picked up the bag and hoisted it over his shoulder, extending out his hand to help her up.

They were almost to the crest of the bowl shaped meadow when Faolan turned to her, looking a bit sheepish.

"Tell me about Miren. Was she in much…pain?"

"That's right; she is your cousin, isn't she?" Faineth smiled and shook her head. "Nah, not much pain at all, really. She was amazing actually; took to her new legs like she had had them all her life."

"Miren has legs. Now that will take some time to get used to," he smiled and giggled a bit before asking another question. "She's happy, then?"

"She was until," Faineth paused, remembering the sight of what happened to the Ocean Clan.

"I am so very sorry for the devastation my uncle has caused your people, Faineth. I truly hope you know that," his words were soft yet pleaded with her at the same time.

"I would never entertain the thought that you or your father or mother had anything to do with it, Faolan." She lowered her head and felt tears in her eyes again, but he nudged her softly and when she looked up, she saw a trail of smoke reaching upward to the heavens.

~ * ~

"I'm still not sure why you need to do this, Ennon. Faolan has delivered us out of that blood bath and now you want to venture out back into it?" Olorin said trying to reason with her only son.

"I'm not going back there, mother, I'm doing something to ensure our kind doesn't die out completely. The less you know, the safer you and Father will be." Ennon said, trying to reassure her. He closed the gap, touching her shoulders softly and kissing her forehead. "It's something I must do and I would appreciate a little faith from you."

"You know you have it, I just don't understand why your father can't journey with you," she said, still pleading for him to change his mind.

"And leave you here all alone? Never," he argued back. "Besides, he would probably follow your wishes and try and stop me."

"Then we will both go with you," she continued.

"And leave an empty house for Faineth to return to? Mother, please see the insanity of which you speak. This must be done and I must do it alone."

"What you speak of is insanity, my son! And just what is it that has you so convinced that this will ensure that our people will live on? You saw them, Ennon, all of them, except for us and by the Maker's grace, your sister, all dead. What kind of magic do you speak of?"

"Not magic, Mother, but I cannot tell you. The less you know, the safer it will be, for all of us. Trust me, please. I can do this. I have done this before. When the threats first started and it worked," he said trying to comfort her.

"What have you done, Ennon," Olorin asked sternly.

"Lower your voice, Mother, you'll wake him," Ennon said, referring to his father that lie sleeping in the next room. His plan was to be gone before he awoke, for he knew his father would never let him leave.

Olorin looked her son in the eyes and whatever she saw at that moment softened her.

"Trust is never a question you should ask, my son," she said as a tear broke loose from her lashes, trailing softly down her cheek. "But you must return to me. I cannot bear a life where my children lived in graves, nor could I bear the wrath of that man on me if you didn't. Promise me, whatever crazy ideas you have running around in that foolish head will see you home safely."

92

"They will, Mother, I swear it," he said and he grabbed his jacket and the small feed sack of food his mother had packed him, thinking he was just going to the field's edge to see if he could see Faolan and his sister. Now, with not knowing how the long his journey might be, she stuffed more food into the make shift pack and threw her arms around him as if it were the last time she would hold her son.

"I promise I will return to you. You have my word," he looked down at her when she pulled away. It was as if she had aged overnight. The fear in her eyes for her family wore at her and showed in her face. There were small lines around her eyes that Ennon hadn't noticed before and it made his heart sink a bit. He hugged her tightly and whispered, "Tell Father I love him, too," and ducked out the door quickly before either of them could change their minds.

11. Reunited

Faolan and Faineth headed down over the hills that had surrounded the Northern range of the Valley of the Mist. It was a rockier, less stable terrain, with an unrecognizable stench that lingered in the air above and Faineth stopped wondering why the safe house would be in a place like this. After all, who in their right mind would stumble upon a place so…unpleasant, purposely, anyways? She looked over at Faolan and wiggled her nose.

"It's just about a half a day's travel that way and I promise, that by the time we arrive, all of this," he said waving his hand in the air, "will be gone. It's a deterrent of sorts. In case they make it this far, my mother thought this would make them turn back for sure," he chuckled. "She said that Wild Heather would invite, whereas decaying boar's head would not."

"This is a spell? Done by your Mother?" Faineth questioned, as a smile spread on her face.

"Yes," he answered looking around as if the smell had just transformed into a beautiful gift from Anya.

"She's pretty amazing. Tell her thank you from me when you see her again, okay?" she said, looking at her friend fondly, but turned at an eerie sound coming from behind them.

"Uh oh, I was afraid of that," Faolan said, grabbing Faineth by the arm picking up speed and almost running.

"Uh oh …what? Faolan, what was that?" she asked, fear lumping in her throat. If the safe house was a half a day's walk ahead of them, it was far enough away from whatever that was that made the sound, but was it too far to get there in time and safely?

"That, Faineth … was the one thing that thinks a decaying Boars head is a delicacy," he said, running a little faster still.

"An Eidolon Goblin?" she half screamed and ran faster, this time almost dragging Faolan along.

"I'm afraid so," he answered and with that, he swooped her up into his arms and shot up into the sky, flying the rest of the way to the safe house.

Arien woke up, feeling groggier than when he had landed on the bed earlier. He couldn't shake the feeling of doom, even though his family, most of them, was safely hidden in this small but nicely built hut. It had been many, many moons since Arien had stayed in one so nice. He lay in the bed looking around, admiring the craftsmanship when he heard it: the soft cries of his wife in the other room. He lifted himself off the bed and put his shirt back on and made a note of washing it before they slept that night, so that it would have time to dry by the fire while they slept.

He walked out to find his wife sitting by the window, alone, and the feeling of doom returned.

"Renny, what is it, woman?" he asked, using his nickname he had given her when they'd first met. A name he only used when they were alone. He crossed the room and softly rubbed her back. The feeling of her husband's worn but loving hands broke whatever strength she was clutching to and she turned and fell into his arms.

"He's gone and there was no stopping him," she whispered through her tears.

Arien stiffened.

"Who's gone?" he asked sternly, but before she could answer the door gave way, practically exploding off the hinges. Their immediate reaction was to scream, but after the dust settled, pure joy washed over them as they embraced the daughter they both were too afraid to admit that they had lost forever.

"Faineth, oh, my sweet Faineth!" cried Olorin. "and Faolan! I've never been so happy to see an Elf in all my life," she shouted out through her tears, tears that had been grief stricken but now were filled with hope. She hugged her daughter tightly, then in an instant, jerked her out at arm's length and looked at her sternly.

"Faineth Seeri R'yor! As your father is my witness if you EVER leave with nothing but a note again, I will not only own your back side, child, I will wear it!" she shouted, but broke away into laughter again, clutching at her child again.

"Words only a mother could speak," Arien laughed and walked over to the both of them, embracing them both. "I will forever be grateful and indebted to you, Faolan."

"I only wish I could have saved more than just you four," he said, looking around. "Where's young Ennon?"

Olorin lifted her head and her face fell again. She turned to her husband then looked down at Faineth, taking a few steps away from her family as if the news she had to tell would cause her to burst into flames.

"He's gone," was all she could say.

"Gone? Gone where? "Arien questioned her, worry and fear pricking at his words.

"I don't know," she whispered, hanging her head in shame. "He wouldn't say, just that I was to trust him and that he had a plan to keep our people from dying out."

"What about my trust? Did he not think to ask for that, as well? Did you not think to have him ask?" Arien began to yell, but

Faolan stepped in trying to diffuse the sudden rage rising in Arien's face.

"Arien, I'm sure he was…," Faolan tried, but Arien continued his questioning.

"We won't really know what he was doing, since the only person who would have insisted an answer was left to sleep! I wasn't even given a chance to stop my son," he shouted; crumbling with admission.

Faineth never thought she would see the day her father would be as broken as he was now. It pained her to see him like this and wondered herself what Ennon was up to. Both her and her mother dropped to his side and hugged him.

"I'm sorry for my harsh words. It is selfish of me to assume that my family, all of my family would be spared from this."

"No apologies needed, Arien." Faolan said, but then looked at Olorin. "When did Ennon leave?"

As soon as he asked it, Faineth knew why. Because of the awful sounds they had heard, sounds of immediate horror if Ennon's path led him straight to the goblins.

"Oh, my," she whispered covering her mouth the minute she said it. "Faolan… if he… if they…,"

"Let's be hopeful Ennon's business took him north," Faolan said, seeing the fear in Ennon's family's eyes.

"What's out there, Faolan?" Arien asked. "What's got you and Faineth worried?"

"A lot of angry, misled, determined Fey folk, but Ennon knew it too, so it is my hope he remembered the way we came and went the other way," he lied, shooting a look in Faineth's direction. She caught on quickly, knowing there was no reason to worry her parents any more than they already were.

"Is anywhere safe? I mean really safe?" Olorin asked as if one of them would have the answer.

"There is no way of really knowing that for sure, but what I do know is that the four of you made it out of there safely for a reason, one I plan on living to see play out," Faolan said, causing the room to relax a bit. He looked at Faineth again and gave a slight nod. "I'll return tomorrow with more food and supplies. You will be safe in here as long as you all stay put. The house is enchanted, so even if someone ventures this way, they won't be able to see it."

"How will my boy know it's here when he returns?" Arien questioned.

"The five of us will see it, past us, it's invisible," Faolan answered giving him a reassuring squeeze on his shoulder.

Faineth knew he was making excuses to go and see if he could find Ennon. If there was a chance he could catch up to him and possibly steer him in the right direction, Faolan was going to take it.

"Thank you, Faolan," Arien said, standing to say goodbye. "May you all be safe, as well."

Faolan gave the three one more look and turned and left. Faineth secretly hoped he would find Ennon in time and that the goblins wouldn't.

~*~

"But it's been three days, Mother," Faineth pleaded with Olorin while cleaning up after breakfast.

"I can't just sit around waiting forever. I have to go and see if I can find them!"

"You'll do nothing of the sort! I can't have two children out wandering the country side like a couple of wood gypsies!" she argued back.

There was still no sign of Ennon or Willow and it was driving Faineth crazy. Her parents didn't think it was safe to go outside, which left her to pace the floors in worry. She didn't know which was causing more stress, either. She knew Ennon could hold his own and really had no idea on where he had gone, so trying to come up with a time frame of when he should return was impossible. Willow, on the other hand, was another story. Faineth didn't know if her little friend was even still alive. The last she had seen of Willow was her flying towards the caves, the same caves that were being invaded by hundreds of misguided elves, with orders from a mad man.

"So we just sit here like stones and wait? Is that your answer, Mother?" Faineth asked in frustration. Her sarcasm would have landed her in trouble before, but her mother knew all too well how she was feeling and let it slide.

"If you can come up with a plan that keeps you safe, I'd be glad to hear it, child, but as it stands, the possibility of only having one child left is haunting my thoughts. I'm not about to entertain the thought of being childless."

Olorin turned and walked into the other room and Faineth knew instantly that the discussion was over, but still it was too hard for Faineth to wrap her mind around her mother's way of thinking. It was always so black and white, cut and dry. She knew there had to be some gray area to consider, but what? She wasn't going to just give up, as it appeared her mother already had done. Faolan had stated that the house was enchanted, so if she left, she wouldn't have to worry about her parent's safety or that she wouldn't be able to find it when she returned. No, the real issue was getting around the goblins and whatever else might be waiting for her in Eidolon Forest.

She too turned and walked into the back bedroom and plopped down on the bed in a motion of defeat, causing it to bounce a bit. It was never in her nature to just give up and wait. That had always been her mother's job. She glanced outside to see her father pacing back and forth nervously, scanning the fields and sky for any sign of life. It warmed her heart to know that he included the dragons in his search. She knew her parents had as much love and respect for the dragons as she did, but with all that had happened, she had wondered if their feelings had changed and it was nice to know they hadn't. Maybe he was the one to talk to about doing something to find Willow, so she gathered up the necessary courage it would take to ask what seemed impossible.

"Any luck?" she asked, joining his nervous pacing. Her words caused him to look around sharply, as if he hadn't heard her approach.

"Oh, Faineth, uh... no, not yet," he answered quickly, returning his attention to his seemingly pointless search.

Faineth saw the intense worry in her father's eyes and decided her conversation could wait. She slipped her smaller, softer hand in his older, worn hand and squeezed.

"He will return, Father. You know Ennon as well as I do. He's the craftiest one out of all of us," she said, trying to ease her father's fear.

"I keep expecting others to walk out of those woods," he said pointing in the direction of Eidolon Forest, "but how could they?"

Faineth dropped her head and tears welled up in her eyes remembering all of the death and destruction she had seen firsthand and knew that what her father was hoping for was pointless. There was no way anyone survived the devastation Faineth witnessed and she knew the only reason her family was spared was because Faolan had gotten to them first.

He was due for a visit the next day, so she decided she would talk with him about a plan to find Willow. She yearned to have the magic of the Fey. To be able to "see" things as they did. She had the gift of sight, but only for the purpose of finding someone or something, not in the way of prophecy like the Elves. It would make things so much easier and thinking about it caused her to think of Melian and all the things she had yet to learn from him about their craft and about the dragons. Fighting back the memories that were starting to flood back, she wiped her tears with the sleeve of her shirt.

"I'm sorry about Willow," her father said softly, interrupting her thoughts. He was looking down at her now, concern for her filled his expression.

"Thank you, Father, but I know she is still out there. I can feel it."

Her father squeezed her hand and looked down at his beloved daughter with so much adoration in his eyes, it almost made Faineth smile.

"You always were the one that had the most hope. Maybe someday we will learn from you," he said, smiling back at her. Faineth watched as a tear broke free of his heavy lashes and made its way down his cheek, leaving a path in the dirt of his skin.

"Father, maybe you should come inside and let Mother draw you a warm bath. It might help you feel better."

"There will be plenty of time for that when your brother is home and safe. Why don't you go and see if she needs any help with supper?" he said, almost choking, trying desperately to hold it together as a sign of strength. The last thing Arien wanted was to fall apart in front of his family. In his mind, as long as he was strong, then they would feel safe and be strong, too. It broke Faineth's heart more witnessing this and she abandoned any hesitation and threw herself into his arms, causing him to let go of the façade and weep deeply as he clung to his daughter.

12. Deceptions

The night air was thick with the smell of death and the warm wind that had come on earlier in the night wasn't helping. The feel of the ground against the soles of her feet was odd. The land felt sticky and wet at the same time. She looked down as she ran towards the caves and came to an immediate stop and covered her mouth to hold back a scream. Her feet were completely covered, from her toes to her ankles. She had been running in pools of blood without even knowing it.

The ground started to spin around her and she felt as if she might fall, but looked back in the direction of where she was headed and the reason of her suicidal journey came flooding back. Willow. Her hand dropped back down to her side and with a thought-cleansing shake of her head, she started to run again. The caves were just up ahead and she was hopeful that Willow was there, still alive.

Noises from the woods surrounding the base of the caves slowed her down a bit and she decided that maybe a more cautious approach would be better. She ducked behind a grouping of bushes to see if she could see what…or who…was making the noise. With no luck, she crawled around, inching her way closer to the caves, but under the cover of the thick vegetation that was once her playground. The ground felt differently than it had before. It felt rougher, somehow, as if the terrain itself had suffered during the battle.

Stopping just short of the entrance to the caves, Faineth noticed two men, or elves rather, standing close to the opening and she knew then it would be virtually impossible to get in without being seen. She would have to come up with another way in or a distraction to get them to leave. She looked around on the ground to see if she could find a rock or smaller stick to throw, but it was too dark so she felt the ground for a lump. It didn't take her long before she felt a rock about the size of an Osprey egg and dug it out with her fingers. Holding it tenderly in her hand, she rose a little on her knees to see where the best place to throw it would be. She wasn't the best aim. That was Ennon's thing, having played on the village's Rugby team: a game brought over by one of the leaders from the human realm.

Deciding on a place just to the left of the caves, Faineth cocked her arm back as far as it would go and let go with as much force as she could muster. The rock cleared the area where the men were standing and crashed into a tree several yards in front of them, sending them running in that direction. She stood and gave a small sigh and bolted for the entrance. If the rock had fallen short, or worse, landed behind them, it would have given her location away and she would have been in trouble. Maybe she should have given Ennon's invitation to play on the team a little more thought, but now was not the time to think of that. That was never to be again.

She rounded the entrance and quickly got inside before the others could return. The entrance was deceiving from the outside. It appeared to have a high ceiling, but once inside, it dropped and if you weren't aware of it, you would find yourself running right into the wall. Lucky for Faineth, she knew these caves all too well and ducked down at the appropriate time. It remained low for about three hundred yards then it opened back up into a large open cavern with many tunnels going off into every direction of the cave. It was in these tunnels the dragons found refuge.

Faineth scanned the area and saw Willow towards the back of the cave and without thinking, she ran as fast as she could to get to her.

"Willow!" Faineth screamed out in joy, at finding her friend relatively easy. But it all changed as fast as it started when Willow slowly turned around, showing signs of being beaten, savagely.

An Elf stood up from behind where Willow had been standing and pulled a large sword that curved at the end, with ornate carvings along the blade. It glistened when the elf brought it around in front of Willow and if it were in any other situation, Faineth would have admired its beauty.

"I've been waiting for you," was all the elf said before bring the blade down, fast and forcibly, across Willow throat, spraying blood in front of her and down her body. Faineth dropped to her knees and screamed out in horrifying pain.

"Faineth… Faineth, child, wake up!" Olorin said, shaking her daughter. Faineth sat up and beads of sweat rolled off her forehead and stung her eyes. It was only a nightmare. She looked around nervously, searching for anything recognizable past her mother, trying to get the image of Willow's murder out of her thoughts.

"What has you so afraid?" Olorin asked.

Faineth looked at her and tried to tell her but the lump in her throat wouldn't let her. Tears flowed freely down her cheeks and she leaned forward, collapsing in her mother's lap. Olorin stroked her hair and whispered "Shh," hoping it would help calm her. She knew she had to pull it together, but the image was still fresh in her mind.

"It was Willow and she was murdered in front of me," was all she could choke out before the tears started to come as if they would never stop.

Knowing of Faineth's abilities of being able to sense things with Willow, Olorin helped Faineth upright again and wiped her tears with her shawl.

"Now, take a few deep breaths and clear you mind and see…" she suggested. "Feel her. Know for sure that's what has happened before you let a dream crush you like this."

Faineth looked at her and knew she was right. She sat up straighter and took a deep breath, coughing from it a bit and closed her eyes, taking a few more breaths before she started to concentrate on Willow. Usually she would see instantly whether or not things were bad, but this time, she felt nothing and it chilled her to the bone. What if it meant she was already gone?

"Relax more, child. You know it won't come if you are upset," her mother offered. She rubbed her arms and it helped Faineth to relax more.

"I'm scared," she whispered. "What if I still can't see her?"

"We will cross that river when we come to it. Now, take another deep breath and this time, concentrate."

Faineth did as her mother said and relaxed enough that her shoulders dropped a bit. She closed her eyes again and thought of nothing but Willow. Images started to flood her mind: thoughts of her and Willow before anything happened and of seeing the dragons fleeing for their lives. She could see the inside of the cave, but unlike her dream, there were other dragons there and best of all… no elves.

She searched deeper in her mind as if she was in the cave with them, searching for any sign of Willow. A glimpse of something white flashed in her peripheral vision and she turned her head. There at the back of cave sat Willow. She was slumped over and she looked hurt, but she was alive. Faineth gasped at what she had seen and opened her eyes.

"She's alive, but she's hurt. I have to go to her, Mother!" she said, almost yelled, and went to get out of bed.

"You'll do nothing of the kind and especially at this hour. Now lie back down and try and get a few more hours sleep. Faolan will be here in the morning and we can ask him to go and get Willow."

"She won't go with him, Mother!" Faineth was screaming and she wasn't worried about waking her father, either. "You don't understand! Almost everything she has known was just destroyed by Faolan's people! The dragons won't let him get close enough to even enter the caves, let alone bring Willow back to me. It must be me, don't you understand?" she pleaded.

"Don't you understand that I can't let you go out there alone, Faineth? Not even for Willow!" she argued back at her daughter and stood to leave. "There will be no other discussion about this, Faineth. You will not be going anywhere. Not for a very, very long time!" Faineth watched as her mother turned and left the small room, leaving Faineth alone again. As compelling as her Mother's argument was, there was no way she was going to listen this time. She had confirmation Willow was alive and after that dream, there was no way she was going to wait any more. She and she alone had to find her and bring her back safely. Her family would just have to understand.

Her biggest concern was getting there. She knew once there, she could ride one of the bigger dragons back to the safe house and if she planned well and left quickly, she might even be lucky enough to be back before her parents had woke up. It was the whole getting past the dread that might be waiting for her in Eidolon Forest thing that was her main concern. She exhaled, thinking about it and scanned the small room that she had made her bedroom, noticing a bag that was propped up in the corner of the room, behind a chair. She got up and retrieved it, tossing it onto the bed to see what it contained. It looked familiar, but she wasn't sure at the moment exactly why.

She fiddled with the ties that kept it shut and opened the flap to reveal the contents, turning it upside down to allow whatever was in the bag to dump out onto the bed. A few apples rolled out and she raised her eyebrows at them fiddling for the larger item that wasn't coming out as easily. As soon as her hand felt it, she smiled. The Elvin Cloak! The very thing that would get her past anything that might have plans for her as their meal of the night. She grabbed it and stood in front of the make shift mirror that hung just above an old wooden chest that was filled with her belongings.

Wrapping it around her shoulders and tugging it close around her neck, she stood back to have a look. Just as she hoped, she was completely invisible from the neck down. Faineth let out a small giggle, holding her hands over her mouth to silence it more. She fluffed the material a bit more to fully wrap around her body so she wouldn't trip on the length and saw a piece of parchment fall to the ground. It was small, but folded neatly and she instantly recognized the wax seal on the back. She broke the seal and opened it slowly glancing over the words inside.

Faineth,

If I know you at all, you will be gone when I return. The bond you and Willow share is much stronger than reason and I fear you will leave to search for her. So, with that being said, I have left you the cloak as a tool you will need, to get you safely back through the forest. As soon as you are through it though, please keep wearing it until you get to the caves. I know it is heavy, but I fear there are still men out there. Please Fain, for me.

Be safe my dearest

friend,

Faolan

Faineth held the note to her chest. She was so thankful for Faolan. It made her sad that more of his people couldn't be like him. She tucked it away in her box, the only thing she really thought of grabbing before leaving her home with Faolan a week earlier and packed a few things in the bag before sneaking out of the room. Once she reached the kitchen, she noticed that she kept tripping up on the length of the cloak, so she didn't think Faolan would mind if she trimmed it a little around the bottom. After trimming it, she tied the extra piece around her bag and it instantly disappeared in her hand.

"Wonderful," she beamed. It actually felt good for her to have something to be happy about. It felt like forever since the last time she had felt that way. She tossed one of the loaves of bread her mother had baked for the morning's supper and jug of water and slung the bag on her back before she wrapped the cloak around her again. She turned and glanced over at the make shift weapons rack her father had finished putting together the morning before and noticed he had added a few things that might be helpful if she did encounter something on her journey. She had been a swordsman in training and her father had been working with her daily before all this had happened, so being titled worthy was yet to be judged. If faced with a battle, her odds were better if she had something to battle with and what she was good with was a bow.

Walking over to the rack to retrieve the long bow her father had added to the collection, she heard footsteps and froze. One of her parents was up and heading in her direction. She hung her shoulders in defeat as her father entered the room, already constructing an excuse for being up and ready for travel. He walked right past her and stood near the table, gazing out the small window that gave light in the day to the kitchen. Faineth went to say something when her father suddenly turned in her direction, but looked right past her before slowly walking back into the bed room, then she remembered. She was still wearing the cloak, all of it and it covered her from head to toe, completely invisible. She sighed deeply, causing her father to turn and look back in the direction of the kitchen. Faineth froze again and watched her father, expecting the worse. But after a quick glance, he continued to the room and shut the door.

She stood motionless for another minute and then let the air out of her lungs.

"So, invisible, but still heard," she muttered to herself as she walked to the front door and opened it. The night air was crisp but tolerable under the heaviness of the cloak. She shut the door quietly, still holding her breath and turned to face the direction of where she must go. A shiver that started at the base of her spine slowly worked its way up to the base of her neck, causing her shoulders to quiver.

"Courage, Faineth, you need to be strong. Willow isn't going to rescue herself," she whispered and took the first step towards Eidolon Forest.

13. Family Business

"How dare you go against my direct order?" Carrig shouted in his brother's face. "You have gone too far this time Roanus! Guards!"

The door to the King's chambers burst open and eight men spilled into the room, surrounding Roanus. None of them would admit it at that moment out loud, but they whole heartedly followed the King and wanted nothing more than to see Roanus imprisoned for his actions.

"You know it had to be done, Brother," Roanus argued, "for Miren's sake."

"No, Father," Miren said walking into the room, causing Roanus to gasp. "What you did to those people and to their families…that was unforgivable." Miren faced her father; her face was void of any emotion.

"Miren, you…you're alive," he whispered, tears welling in his eyes. "I did this all for you. To make sure you would always be safe."

"Don't you dare put the blood of those innocent people on my head!" she screamed. "That stain is yours and yours alone to bear!"

"Innocent? Has everyone in this room gone mad? Do we not remember our brother, your hand," he said, shooting a piercing glance in the direction of Carrig.

"Of course we remember, Belamros! But instead of holding the Guardian responsible for his disappearance and possible death, you, the true mad man, order an entire race of people and creature to be completely annihilated," Carrig shouted back and it seemed as if the whole room reverberated at his voice. Anya had never heard her husband speak this way and she rose from the chair she had been sitting in and went to his side.

"Roanus, what you have done is contemptible," she spoke softly, controlled.

"Guards, take this man to the dungeons. He will be tried for treason in the morning," Carrig said and he thought he felt his heart actually break a bit. He had already lost one brother and now with his other brother's actions, it looked as if he would be brother-less in a very short time. He turned towards his wife, avoiding any further eye contact with Roanus and lifted his hand to stroke her cheek. Anya smiled softly at him, her eyes showing only love and support.

"You will regret this! You will see someday I was right in what I did!" Roanus yelled to his family. Miren looked at him with pity.

"I have never understood you, Father, and I don't begin to try to now," she said, stopping any further rants he might have. You could almost see Roanus break at her words and he hung his head as the King's guards dragged him off. One thing that no one ever questioned, other than Miren herself, was the love that he had for her. His actions of showing it, however, would have never stood on their own as proof. The doors shut as soon as they were out of the room and Miren turned towards her aunt and uncle and finally let her true feelings show.

"You belong to this family now, my dearest Miren," Anya said, wrapping her arms around the crying Miren.

"That will never change," Carrig added, wrapping his large arms around the both of them, when Faolan walked into the room. By the look on his face, he must have passed his uncle on the way to see his father.

The king looked up to see his son and tried to smile.

"Are they safe?" he asked and the women looked up and then towards Faolan.

"Is who safe?" Miren questioned.

"Yes, for the most part they are. With the exception of Ennon," Faolan answered his father first then addressed Miren's question. "I have delivered the R'yor's to the safe house. I got there just in time, too. Faineth was about to meet with some of your men when I-" Faolan's words were stopped with Miren's gasp.

"Faineth is okay? She's alive," she questioned and she smiled through more tears, only this time, they were tears of joy. "Oh, Faolan! She's really alive?"

"Yes, cousin, she is safe and sound, as promised," he smiled back at her.

"Tell me, Son, what does 'for the most part' entail?" the king questioned, looking worried.

"Ennon has left and for now, no one knows where he has traveled or what has caused him to do so. Olorin had said it was something he felt he needed to do to help their people from dying out, but I think it may be too late for that, now. They are the last of their kind. If Ennon or Faineth mate, it will not be a pure line and I'm not sure if that will change things for the remaining dragons, if there are any remaining dragons," he said, trailing off in thought. For a moment, the room fell silent as if everyone was processing what he said.

"He did it," the king said softly, almost a whisper and Faolan looked at him.

"Did what?" Faolan walked over closer to Carrig and bent his head slightly to look his father square in the eye. "Tell me, Father, what do you know?"

Carrig looked up at his son and then looked at Miren, finally settling on Anya's face. A wide smile spread across his face and he started to laugh through the tears, clapping his hands.

"He did it!" he shouted victoriously.

~*~

"Aisling, you have to help me," Ennon pleaded with the tiny pixie fairy, a close friend to the Baelian's and now a close friend to Ennon's family, as well.

"I don't see as to how this will help…not like it's gonna get ya a mate," the little fairy said, landing on the branch of the tree Ennon was standing next to. She put her hands on her tiny hips to add to her argument.

"I'm not looking for a mate," he argued back.

"Oh, no…I know. You are just lookin' to knock up some poor unfortunate human so yer people don't die out. Didn't ya hand me that same speech a few weeks past and didn't I deliver for ya?"

"Yes, but it must be done again. It didn't…work… last time and you better than anyone knows the timing is different there. I won't be noticed, I assure you. I have figured out what I must do this time."

"Time, shmime! Yer plan is going to get ya in trouble with the king!" Aisling spouted off, knowing this would end it.

"Well, now, that's where you are wrong, little friend. I actually have the King's support on this," he said smiling.

"You… what? There's no way Carrig will ever support this! No way! I can't believe ya would even try and trick me like this!" she shouted in a frenzy, lifting off the tree and flying around Ennon's head as she bickered. Ennon let her lecture him, as he pulled a letter from his left pocket and unfolded it, lifting it in front of her, causing her to run into it. The tiny fairy slammed into the parchment and bounced off of it, spinning back towards the tree. Ennon lifted his hand to catch her before she actually hit it.

113

Holding her tight enough that an escape wasn't possible, but that he wasn't hurting her either, Ennon read what it said to her.

Ennon,

As mad as your idea sounds, I have decided to grant you my full support and protection. May the Maker's grace and guidance be always with you,

King Baelian

Aisling read it too and her face softened.

"You could 'ave just told me instead of lettin me smash into it," she scolded. "Fine, it's yer neck that's on the line," she pouted, but Ennon knew this was her way of saying she was worried. He lifted his hand that held her to his lips and he kissed the top of her tiny head. She squirmed in his hands and squawked.

"If I was to take ye there…again… what's in it for me?"

Ennon smiled slowly.

"What is it that you want? My resources aren't as… limitless as they once were," he stated, thinking of the amount of loss he had been through in a few short days.

"I'll get back to ya on that. We best be goin if you wanna make it through undetected," she said and he let her go. She flew up and landed on his shoulder and Ennon walked in the direction of the portal.

"I hope yer right and this works, Ennon. You're pretty crazy, ya know."

"It will, Aisling. It has to."

14. Well Laid Plans

The sound of the cell door unlocking rang out in Roanus' ears and he wrinkled his face. The bigger of the two guards that were holding his arms threw him forward into the belly of the cell and locked the door behind him.

"I know your names," he said without turning in their direction. "And when my brother comes to his senses and releases me, I will have each one of you executed," he continued, slowly turning in the direction of the door, facing the guards. "And I will do it myself."

The guards looked at him and then broke out into laughter. One from the back walked forward and pressed his face to the bars of the door.

"Then it will be the first time any of us have seen a ghost, as you will die at sunrise, Roanus. The orders have already been given. Looks as if your brother has already come to his senses," the guard known as Peadar answered, smiling.

Roanus looked at him and tried not to show the pain in his heart. To be completely cut off from the King this way was not what he was expecting. He was expecting to spend a few nights down here then be called to discuss things with his brother. Between Miren's lack of feelings towards him and now this… it was more than he could bear and he sunk to the ground. The guards laughed at him and one even spit at him, then turned and left the dungeons. It was so dark in the cell, he didn't notice he had company until it was sitting directly in front of him.

"Sad when family is like that," it said. "They call me Borlaug," he said, after seeing the man jump at the sound of his voice.

"What are you? I can't even see you," Roanus asked angrily.

"You elves are all the same, aren't you," the creature named Borlaug lectured. "You have given yourselves such an air of importance, that all fall short of your glory," he continued to mock. "I am a Changeling, if you must know, as if it makes a difference now," he answered.

"A...Changeling, they locked me up with a Changeling?" Roanus mocked back. "My brother really does hate me." A snicker escaped Roanus and he noticed his eyes were starting to adjust to the lack of light. The creature's silhouette, which was sitting closer than he first thought, came into view. He moved back a bit, not really wanting to be too close.

"I'm not going to bite you, it's just been a while since I have had any company," Borlaug apologized with a tone of sarcasm.

"How long have you been here?"

"Since right before the summer solstice, but it's a blur to the actual day."

"That's a long time," Roanus stated, thinking more about how long his stay was and how little he would have to put up with his cell mate.

"Rumor has it that I will be out by morning. The king thinks I have served my time and that I'm... reformed," the Changeling smiled. Roanus couldn't see him clearly, but he knew there was a smirk on his face.

"What was it that you have done to have angered my Brother so much that he has had you in here for that long without an execution?"

"What we are so famous for, of course. Only this time, I swapped the wrong child."

Roanus knew all too well what they were capable of, having known a few and having asked them for favors. Changelings were vile creatures, really, and not just because they resembled smaller, more haggard fairies such as a brownie or a gnome, but for the things they did. They would soon take your soul for a rabbit pelt, just as they would laugh at a joke. They were, after all, the most atrocious of the Fey.

"You messed up on a trade, yet you live. Interesting," Roanus baited. He knew Changelings were almost as vain as they were evil, given the opportunity to brag, they would jump on it.

"Well, now, you see, that is where your brother should have applauded me, yet instead, he imprisoned me," Borlaug bragged, taking the bait that Roanus had laid in front of him. "It was so masterfully done, that it was only discovered recently that a mistake had happened. It's silly, really. I was to swap with one of Nefaran's spawn and instead took an innocent child."

The wizard Nefaran that Borlaug was speaking of was not well liked in Ethreal. The rumor had always been that he was appointed head Wizard to the King's court by the Maker himself, but the power that entailed was too enticing and it turned him evil. No one would go anywhere near him for a while and it was said that he had disappeared, until one of the pixies on a routine trip to the human world, saw him with a maiden. After returning with more of her kind, it was discovered that he had been crossing over a lot, impregnating innocent human women along the way, only to leave them alone with an evil child to parent.

"And just how was it discovered?" Roanus asked, baiting for more information.

"The Lady Breaga had foreseen the child that I was supposed to take. She had told the Queen Anya of its evil and the Queen herself hired me, granting me free passage to the higher grounds when it was over, so that I would be safe," he laughed in jest. "Safe...," he patted the cell floor with the palms of his hands, "just look where safe landed me."

Lady Breaga, Roanus thought, was a dear friend to the Queen and a very powerful witch, or so most said. If you asked Anya, she would say that Lady Breaga was just blessed in the gift of Prophecy.

"Like I said, you are lucky to be alive. Nefaran is force to reckon with." Roanus inched back till he found the wall and leaned against it. "Whatever became of this child, the one you were supposed to dispose of?"

"Rumor has it he is like a court jester in a place called Las...something, I forget. It feels as if it's been a thousand moons since I have crossed over. Starts with a V..." he said, still thinking.

"How did you get caught? You, of all Changelings, one so crafty, that our very Queen seeks your favor herself?"

"See, even you know of my talents," Borlaug bragged on, not knowing that Roanus was merely enticing him to tell him the whole story. He wondered if Borlaug thought he was going to die tomorrow, maybe he would share something with him, that the King and Queen was not aware of and it would be the bargaining chip he would need to spare his life.

"It was your other brother, what was his name?" Borlaug asked sarcastically. He knew all too well who Belamros was. Roanus glared at him and almost said something in return, but Borlaug continued. "He was over there, seeing that wench he was claiming to love. If you ask me, he was just looking for a way out of his arrangement. He saw the boy and happened to mention it to the Queen and the rest is history," he said, lifting his feet high enough the shackles around his ankles rattled.

Roanus ignored his snide remarks about his family. It really wasn't worth the effort, as far as he was concerned. He let his head fall back onto the wall behind him and shut his eyes.

"Tell me, Roanus," Borlaug said, interrupting his idea of quiet. "What has happened to land you here?"

"That's none of your business," Roanus said sharply.

"What, no last confessions to cleanse your soul? No washing the spirit clean of evil doings? I'm shocked…," the Changeling taunted him.

"According to the Queen, I have no soul to cleanse."

"Hmm, must have been some to do if that is how she feels. Do tell Roanus. I've had so little…entertainment as of late," he snickered.

Roanus shut his eyes and thought of the Queen's face and the look of total disgust in her eyes for him. That was the one thing about all he had been through that had truly broken his heart. It was a hard thing to bear, the total disappointment she had for him. Truly, Miren and her sister had left him many moons ago emotionally, so the part of losing his family was nothing in comparison to losing Anya's affection. It was never the kind he had secretly hoped for, but any feelings she had for him, even if it were only friendship, was better than this.

He laughed. "I had an entire race of people and their *pets* annihilated," he whispered.

"An entire race, you say?" Borlaug asked, but it sounded more like he was prodding Roanus, now.

"Yes, an entire race," he replied.

"And are you sure it was the …entire…race?"

Roanus lifted his head once more and was surprised to see how much his eyes had adjusted with the lack of light. He could see Borlaug perfectly, right down to the smirk on his face.

"Yes, Borlaug, I'm sure," he spat back.

"It's just that I thought I overheard of the tragedy, but also thought I heard that some, well, one family to be specific, actually made it to a safe house, so to speak. I may have heard other things, as well, but if you say it was an entire race, why then, of course, I would tend to believe you."

Roanus glared at Borlaug. His snide remarks and self-righteous behavior made him want to add him to the list of casualties.

"What did you hear and from who?"

"Oh, I heard a little of… this and that. You know how word travels down here. No one figures on anyone spreading the information so they all speak freely. Guess no one heard that I was to be released." He practically beamed telling this to Roanus. Roanus was growing tired of his vain banter and decided enough was enough.

"Tell me what you know and you will be released as planned. Bore me any further with your pride and I will see to it that you hang alongside me, am I clear?" he said sternly, leaning out away from the wall, towards Borlaug.

"Perfectly, your grace," he hissed. "It seems, the King and Queen have taken a particular liking to a certain Guardian family by the name of R'yor. Maybe you know them?" he taunted.

"I know only one, but by first name. I know no one by that name."

"Ah, but I think the one you know may be connected to the ones they know. You see, this family had a daughter, a very talented daughter, who knew her craft well."

Roanus sat up a little straighter still and Borlaug knew he had his full attention.

"I think they mentioned the daughter's name as well. Let me see if I remember it," he said, rubbing the edge of his chin.

"Faineth, her name is Faineth," Roanus answered, anger welling up in his soul.

"Yes! I knew I would remember as soon as I heard it. So they're one in the same then?"

"She was the reason I did what I did," Roanus said, admitting to half of his plan, leaning back against the wall in total defeat. His head was spinning and he felt as if he would pass out. To know that all of what had happened was in vain, that nothing he had set out to accomplish had actually happened was the final straw. He would go to his death willingly in the morning. There was nothing left for him to live for.

"And why may I ask did you send orders for all of them to be destroyed? It must have been pretty awful for you to make a decision so destructive."

"She made an abomination out of my daughter, not to mention they killed my brother, the hand to the King. They had to be stopped."

"Well, I guess you did in a way slow them down. The brother seems to have a different idea, though," he said and his vagueness of his words caused the blood to boil in Roanus' veins.

"Tell me what you know, Borlaug! NOW!" he shouted and caused the Changeling to jump a bit.

"No need for yelling, Roanus, all you needed was to ask," he replied, gathering his senses again.

"There is an old prophecy I had thought died long ago. But with these latest events, I'm starting to wonder. I heard another...uh...rumor that our young Ennon, Faineth's brother, has been sneaking visits to the human world and let's say, planting his seed as well? I guess Nefaran wasn't the only one playing creator in Ethreal, although, so far it's only been twice and the first time failed, but I heard a few hours before they put you in here that this last attempt was successful. There should be a baby on the horizon in no time. Of course, its powers in comparison will be weak, but nevertheless, it will be half Guardian and will possess the gifts of their people, just as the prophecy foretold."

"What prophecy do you speak of, Borlaug? Do not waste my time," Roanus demanded.

"It was told long ago, that a young girl, a Halfling or mixed blood, so to speak, from a lesser standing would come alongside a man of power and upset the balance of our realm. In other words...destroy the true man of power, the one that wiped out her people and so on and so forth. See the resemblance?"

"This can't be. They should not be allowed to live after what they have done and I have never heard of such prophecy. I think you are making it up. Wouldn't be the first time you have used trickery to get what you want," Roanus argued and hung his head, closing his eyes. It rang too true. He had wanted to upset the balance for many years to try and gain power in Ethreal. He had always thought it was he that should have been King, not his weak brother, Carrig, and he should have Anya. Getting rid of a race that most of Ethreal thought of as evil was how he hoped to accomplish what was rightfully his. Belamros just helped him see that. Keeping up the appearance that he was truly sickened by what had happened to his brother was all an act.

"Pity you went to all that trouble and caused so much destruction with really no results for you personally, Roanus. I can't imagine how that must feel, but what I say is true. Interpret it how you may, the likeness is too much for me to ignore," he said, void of true feelings behind his words. "Too bad you are to die tomorrow. We may have been able to fix that little problem together," he said nonchalantly, taunting Roanus again.

"There is no fix to this...this mess I have created. I have done so much, yet achieved nothing," he said softly, eyes closed, still refusing to fully believe his so called prophecy.

"Oh, now come, things are never really truly finished, are they Roanus? Especially if they still exist. Why, all you have to do is ask and I may have something I can do for you, to ensure you go to the grave with no regrets that is."

"Sure you can," he whispered. This time it was his turn to be sarcastic.

"Think, Roanus. What is the one thing that could happen now that you would feel… justification? What's the one thing you could do or ask," he lingered on the word, "for that would help you get revenge, help you feel as if you have accomplished what you set out to do and eliminate the prophecy of your own destruction?"

"Well, for starters…" he started to say, then opened his eyes and looked directly at Borlaug. "You would do that? I have nothing to offer you."

"Ah, but you do. If I recall, you have a very special article that belonged to the Queen. Am I correct for thinking this? If I was to say, get my hands on that, it may come in handy someday."

Roanus looked up at him again. How could he know that he had it? No one besides he and Anya knew that he did. It was so long ago that she had given it to him and it was only out of friendship that she had, but Roanus clung to it in hope, as he believed Anya never told Carrig that she had and it made Roanus think that she had feelings for him as well. Truth was that he knew and had told Anya to give it to Roanus, in hopes that it would protect his brother someday. Anya's feelings, in reality, had never extended past a brotherly love for Roanus.

He thought hard for a few minutes tossing around the proposition that had just been laid at his feet. If Borlaug would take care of the baby, it would ensure the Guardian's extinction. That alone was worth giving up the one thing he had held onto for so long, regardless of some tall tale Borlaug was trying to sell him. He sighed deeply and looked once again at his cell mate.

"It will be a bit of a trick for you to get, as I'm sure most of my things will be destroyed once I am gone, but it's yours if you will take care of the child," he said dryly.

"Wonderful decision, my lord," he beamed. The idea of something like this waiting for him when he got out and knowing he would have a tool if he was to be caught again, caused him to smile. "You have my word it will be done."

"Well, then you will need to know where to go to find it," Roanus said, motioning for Borlaug to come closer and the two huddled together for what would become Roanus' final orders.

15. When Legends Fall Short

The night air was colder than Faineth had expected and she wondered if it wasn't part nerves. She really only had stories of the things that lived in the forest to go on, having slept through the journey on Faolan's back the first time through. She didn't know what was scarier; the monsters in the tall tales told by the old clansmen around open fires during festivals, or the fact that she really didn't know what to expect. Most always, she thought to herself, experience is best, but she was hopeful this one time it wouldn't matter as she turned in the direction of Eidolon Forest.

She reached the craterlike meadow that she and Faolan had stopped in and turned and looked back in the direction of the cabin. It was dark and even though the night sky was littered with stars above, the moon was nowhere to be found, so visibility wasn't good. She could make out the silhouette of the hills, but that was it. She sighed deeply, realizing she was past the protection of Faolan's spell and thankful that since it was in the middle of the night, the likelihood of someone seeing her was slim.

Cinching the cloak more securely around her, she turned back towards the forest, practicing walking as quietly as she could.

"Must not make a sound," she murmured as she walked. "Must not talk," she scolded herself, then stopped and looked around. It was still a ways away from the tree line, but she could feel herself getting more nervous as she got closer.

"This is no use," she sighed again. She looked up at the stars again, hoping to see any sign of dragons, without any luck. Her mind filled with visions of what she had seen in her village, but she quickly altered it, with a shake of her head, into something more productive. Instead of fear and pain, she imagined strength and courage. She wouldn't help Willow, after all, carrying on like a sissy child, she thought. She adjusted her bag under the cloak, making sure that every part of her was secure and pressed on. She was a Guardian, after all. What could she face in those trees that she would not be able to handle? Absolutely nothing.

She got within a few paces of the trees when the howling started. It wasn't close, but it still caused the hairs on the back of her neck to rise at full attention. She reached under her cloak for the bow and remembered she hadn't actually taken it off the rack. She had been distracted by her father and had left before realizing she hadn't yet retrieved it. All she was worried about, at the time, was getting out of the house undetected.

"It's now or never, Faineth," she whispered to herself and she stepped through the trees. Wishing she could close her eyes till she reached the other side, she kept them on the mossy ground under her feet. After about fifty steps in, she noticed she was holding her breath. Stopping, she closed her eyes and lifted her head to try and inhale as quietly as possible. She figured if she didn't see anything then the fear wouldn't return, but then remembered she was supposed to be brave and let her eyes open.

With them open ever so slightly, she looked around. Surprisingly, it was beautiful. Opening them fully, she took in her surroundings. Instead of the horrific picture of swamp, slime, and stench, it was mossy, soft, and intoxicating. It was brighter inside the trees, not fully daylight bright, but bright enough to make out the forest around her, thanks to what looked like tiny candles tucked so neatly into place, as if they had grown with the rest of the vegetation, but the oddest part was the flame appeared to be glowing water.

Even though it was approaching winter, there were flowers hanging in the trees and littered on the ground like a hand woven carpet. The moss was a beautiful shade of green, not the sickly yellow she had imagined in her mind. The trees were lush with growth, not twisted and dead like she had pictured. It even felt warmer than it had outside the tree line. She shook her head a little, as if she was trying to wake from a dream.

"This can't be," she whispered.

126

"And why not?" answered a voice.

Faineth froze and quickly looked around in all directions, but saw nothing.

"Well, we are waiting to hear your answer," whispered another voice in a different direction.

"You would think being a *Guardian* and all, she would be a little more garrulous," whispered a third voice.

"Oh, see, now, you just learned that word a few moons ago and already you are trying to sound too smart for the rest of us, it's rude," came a fourth voice.

Faineth went from being scared to being amused and let a giggle escape her lips.

"And now she's laughing at us. Wonderful, just wonderful," said the first voice again.

"It might help if I knew who I was laughing at," she answered.

As if they materialized before her eyes, several men, women, and children stood before her, in a circle, the tallest being close to the same size as Faineth. They were friendly looking enough that she reached up and took the hat of the cloak off, revealing her head.

"Oh, we could see you with it on, you know. Those don't work with us," one of the taller women standing to her side spoke up. "Let me introduce myself, my name is Hattantia Peraladonus, but you can call me Hattie." The woman held out her hand, in a very proper fashion, for Faineth to shake.

Faineth noticed that Hattie had wide set eyes and oversized nose and ears, much like a dwarf, but these beings were softer, somehow. For one, they didn't have the wrinkled weathered skin of a dwarf. Their skin was almost luminescent or pearly with freckles like tiny diamonds on their cheeks. They weren't necessarily fat like dwarves either, although Hattie looked as if she had had her fair share of sweets in her life. Their clothing was humble, but had a magical look to it, as if the fabric glowed.

"Hello, it's very nice to meet you, Hattie," Faineth answered, shaking her hand, which felt smooth in hers. "My name is Faineth."

Hattie noticed the look on Faineth's face. "Is there anything wrong, my dear," she asked, stepping a bit closer towards her.

Faineth looked down at her and smiled. "I just didn't expect you, is all."

"Were you expecting goblins and werewolves and evil wizards?" asked one of the men in the crowd, grinning and rubbing his hands together in anticipation, that caused Faineth to giggle again.

"Well, goblins, yes, but not the wizards and werewolves. Are there even werewolves here?" Faineth asked and the man who asked started to smile wide and clap.

"Yes... I told you, Golthamaur! I told you it would work!" he shouted as he circled the group, clapping as he was shouting.

"Don't be a braggart, Micas! I didn't say it *wouldn't* work, I just merely said it needed a little fine tuning and I was right," argued the man named Golthamaur. "She only heard goblins, which means it needs fine tu-" he continued but was cut off.

"Fine tune, me arse! Golthy! You saw her; she was scared as stone when she heard us. That's more than we could have hoped for," he said, slowing down and coming to a stop right in front of Faineth. He was one of the smaller men and when he looked up at her and smiled, she giggled at his almost toothless grin. "To fool one so wise, that's much, much more than I could have hoped for."

"Now don't go and scare her off, Micas, she probably has loads of questions for us, as well," Hattie said, shooing Micas back into the crowd. "Are ya hungry, lassie? I've just taken a pot of

Honey Tea off the fire and I've a basket full of mountain berry biscuits fresh from the morning's baking. The bottom ones might still be warm," she continued with a hopeful grin, as she guided Faineth deeper into the forest. She turned to look at the rest of the crowd, but most seemed to have dispersed, with only a few following behind. She wondered if it was to see what she would have to say or if it had to do with Hattie's biscuits.

They walked for what seemed a while when the trees opened up before them, revealing several small houses that were stacked on top of one another. It was as if they were built around the trees themselves, circling upward, much like a ribbon wrapped around a maypole, with gaps between them big enough to allow for the spiral staircase that allowed the people to travel from home to home. The stairs themselves looked to be part of the trees, with vines intertwining into what was a rail to hold while climbing. The steps appeared to have grown straight out of the tree, each one perfectly level. The houses looked as if they floated in midair, only connecting to the trees by the vine railings. She counted fourteen trees with these houses built onto them before Hattie interrupted her thoughts.

"Come now, dearie, plenty of time to study our architecture when your belly's full," she said, tugging on Faineth, pulling her in the direction to one of the trees in the back. As they passed the others, she noticed little faces peeking out the windows, watching her as she walked by. Children, she thought and locked in on one face and smiled. Round, soft, pudgy cheeks with rosy, soft lips smiled back at her and as quickly as she noticed her, she was gone from the window, but the giggling that resonated from the open window filled the air.

"That's little Cora. She'll be pestering you by the time the sun's up," Hattie said without looking back at the child or her house. It was as if she had eyes on the back of her head.

"Speaking of the sun," Faineth questioned, picking up her pace to match Hattie's. "Don't you sleep?"

"Yes, yes, we do sleep," Hattie answered looking at Faineth with a furrowed brow. "But it's not sleep season yet, it would be silly for us to sleep now. Who would do all the work?" The way she questioned Faineth was as if she should have known this if nothing else.

"Sleep *season?*"

Hattie stopped and was shaking her head. "Pfft! Have ye no idea who you've stumbled upon lassie? We're Wood Gnomes, we have seasons, surely you've heard of us?" she continued when the puzzled look on Faineth's face did not go away. "You are a sheltered one then, aren't ya."

"Something like that," Faineth answered.

"Well, then quick lesson on Wood Gnomes. We have sleep seasons, we are the peace keepers not peace makers of the realm, we don't cause no trouble, unless you are meaning to do evil in these woods, then you best be smart like and leave before we retaliate, see," she rattled on, as they walked further. Faineth continued to take in her surroundings, missing more than half of the detailed description of, her newest friend's people. "We like to keep to ourselves mainly, but take on a visitor or two," she persisted, looking back at Faineth and winking, pulling her attention back to her lecture. "Now then, any questions?" Hattie opened the small door to the bottom house and turned back towards Faineth, inviting her in with an expression.

Before she stepped inside the, what appeared too small of a house for her to fit, she did think of one.

"Is that why Midas…" she started but Hattie corrected her immediately.

"Micas, lassie, best not make that mistake in front of him. He can be an awful grump."

"Sorry, Micas, is that why he has the woods enchanted? Is it why he makes the sounds of the goblins, to steer folks away?"

"Only the bad ones, lassie, only the bad. Now, how about that cup of tea, huh?"

Faineth smiled, feeling happy she wasn't one of the bad ones and stepped inside the small hut, only noticing it wasn't so small once inside. She looked around in awe as she was able to stand fully upright. From the outside, the huts looked smaller than her mother's potting shed back in their village. From the inside, it looked ten times that big.

"Is this some kind of magic?" she asked Hattie, who was already in the other room pouring tea and placing, what Faineth thought to be, the prettiest little biscuits she had seen on a plate that was decorated with flowers.

"Humm? What was that?" Hattie asked, entering another room off to the side, placing the tray of goodies down on a quaint little table.

Faineth ignored her inquisition to what she had said and continued to gaze around at the house. It was done in very colorful, but not really matching, patterns and colors, but it all seemed to go together to make it cute. It was definitely cozy enough, she thought, not really remembering a time when she had seen this much color in one place. The same odd watery candles filled the rooms with soft light just as they did outside the hut. There were so many things to look at, too. It would take her literally all day to take it all in. Hattie, as it turned out, was quite the collector of pretty little things.

She walked over to a small hutch in the corner that had shelves stacked on top of it, fitting perfectly into the corner without any gaps behind it. Sitting on each shelf, displayed in all of their glory, were tiny hand carved wooden animals. Whoever had made them was a very talented person, as they were easily recognizable. Faineth smiled wide when she saw the Sea Eagle towards the back of the collection. It was a bird that made her think of her brother. Large, bold, masculine, and fearless, just like Ennon.

"Golthy made 'em for me," Hattie said, standing directly behind Faineth, causing her to jump. "Oh, sorry, dear, thought you heard me."

"Golthy?" Faineth questioned, silently willing her heart back into her chest.

"Golthamaur Scubs, haughty little man he is. Has a sweet spot for me, he does, which I refuse to return, you see, but he keeps making me these," she added as her words softened and her hands touched them lovingly.

"Do you have a favorite?" Faineth asked.

"Well, I suppose I do," she said reaching into the back of the second shelf and pulling out a small kitten. "Purdy."

"Yes, she is pretty," Faineth smiled.

"No, dear, that's her name… Purdy. She was a mangy little thing, but loved her, I did. She was laid to rest about a year or so ago and Golthy made this 'un for me to remember her by."

"That was nice of him," she added, looking down at Hattie, who was neatly tucking it back into its rightful place.

"Not nearly so nice that it should be making me about to consider all the offers, mind you, but yes, it was nice. How about you, dear? Any of these you see might be to your liking?"

"It would have to be that one, I think," Faineth said pointing to the larger bird.

Hattie stretched up on her tippy toes and reached for the sculpture and placed it in Faineth's hands. "Of course it would be. Then it's only right it should belong to you now," she smiled. "Maybe Golthy knew you were coming when he made it, it is my newest, after all."

"Would he?" Faineth asked, looking away from the tiny figurine sitting in the palm of her hand. "Can you…do Wood Gnomes have the gift of prophecy?"

132

"Yes, dearie, we do." Hattie stepped back and took a good look at Faineth. "You really haven't ever heard of us, have you?"

"No, sorry, but please don't be offended by it. I haven't really met many folks past my own clan."

"Oh," she laughed, "I'm not offended, just curious…very curious, indeed." She turned and walked back towards the table that held the tray of goodies on it and sat in the extra-large sofa, making the dust puff around her as she landed on the cushions. "Come sit, these biscuits are cold now, not as good, mind you, but it will still help those grumblings your belly is about to produce."

The minute she said the words, Faineth's stomach growled. She giggled at her new friend and sat next to her on the couch, that wasn't nearly as large for Faineth as it was for Hattie.

"We have things to discuss," Hattie started, pouring a cup of sweet smelling tea and handing it to Faineth. She mindlessly went to touch the flame of one of the water candles that sat on the table next to them in a very ornate candle stick. "Mind yourself, child. They're hotter than one would think."

"We do?" Faineth asked, pulling her hand away from the bizarre flame and grabbed one of the biscuits, that she noticed were light pink in color and setting it on her flowered plate, before accepting the tea from Hattie.

"My lands, child! I would just as soon decide you left the house this night with your mind still in the bread basket, if I thought that were even possible," she laughed out loud and Faineth couldn't help but laugh along with her. There was something about these people that struck Faineth oddly, but liking them, she was finding out, was a very easy thing to do. "Let's not forget the wee one, shall we?"

Faineth looked up just in time to see the small child Hattie had called Cora peeking through the window across from her, drop down out of sight. "Oh, yes, let's invite her in. I won't eat all of these," she answered, but when she went to grab another biscuit, Hattie grabbed her hand and looked her square in the face.

"Not that wee one, lassie. She's had enough of my biscuits to choke a magpie. It's Willow I be talking about," she said in a hushed, more serious tone.

Faineth sat up straight as if she had been pulled out of a trance. She could feel tears well up and she forced herself to swallow the small bite of biscuit that she suddenly seemed to be choking on with the thought of Willow. It was as if this place had completely wiped out any plan of rescue from her mind and she was consumed with guilt by her actions. What if Hattie hadn't said anything? Would she have ever left?

"What trickery is this?" she demanded angrily and she went to stand up, but Hattie still had a firm grip around her wrist, pulling her back down on the couch.

"Trust me, child, you go running off after her now and you will do nothing good for either one of you. You *need* our help," she said sternly, softening her grip on Faineth once she felt her relax.

"Help? Help me how?"

"Well, for starters, you will need to know exactly where she is. You can't go traipsing around while there are madmen out there looking to destroy you, unless you have a plan already. I don't want to be all presumptuous and think you don't have one. That would be rude," she said, fully knowing she had none.

"My plans were to get to the caves, get her out and return to the cabin where the rest of my family is," Faineth said almost too fast for Hattie to catch it all.

"Is there another way to get to the caves without going straight through your village, lass?"

"Yes, but only by way of dragon," she answered then looked back up at Hattie.

"And do ye have one of them around to help ya now?" Hattie asked, already knowing the answer, but hoping the question would prove her theory on Faineth needing help.

"Well, no, not right now. I was kind of hoping I would find some along the way, to be truthful," she weakly admitted. It was oddly like sitting across from her mother right after getting caught in the sweet berry pie.

"Exactly my point, dearie. No traipsing, not while I'm around. Now, where were we? Oh yes, saving the wee one." Hattie pulled some parchment and what look like a burnt twig from behind her skirts, looked at Faineth and smiled wide enough that all of her teeth showed.

16. Friendship

"Ennon!" shouted Aisling when she saw him approach the portal. " I thought ya'd gone off and got yerself caught!"

"Now…why would I…go off and do that, eh, Aisling?" Ennon answered, out of breath from running.

It had been three days since she had seen him go through the portal to do what he needed, but knowing that time was different in comparison, she really didn't know when to expect him and was starting to fear she would need to cross over herself to keep him safe.

"Well?" she asked, smacking his shoulder as she flew closer. Ennon just laughed, having not felt the gesture at all.

"Well what? Did I accomplish what I had set out to do? Yes," he smiled, seeing her thankful reaction. "What? You doubted me? *Me*?" he teased.

"It's jus I never have supported crazy stuff like this, you thinkin' you needin to go and spread the love around like some wild dog," she teased back.

"Wild dog, is it? I can own that," he smiled. "More like a few enchantment potions and little switch of the sam…"

"Eww! Don't go off and share any details!" Aisling shouted, thoroughly disgusted in what she thought was coming next in his story. "Besides…it's not natural," she added, staking claim to a spot on his shoulder to sit the remainder of their journey.

"Maybe not, but it's what had to be done," Ennon answered in a softer voice. The recent trip was successful, but that didn't take away from what had happened, to the people he knew and loved and the dragons. This was the only way he could think of to save his people from completely becoming extinct, even if something ended up happening to his family, the Guardians would live on.

"Was it…weird?" Aisling asked cautiously. She wanted to know what it was like, just not any of the details.

"Not sure I would use the word weird," he answered. "More like awkward."

"Well, of course it would be, ya daft rod! I mean, ya have to pull out the…" she started, but he stopped her before she could go any further.

"I thought we agreed on no details," he asked, with a nervous giggle. "Spare me the details of how you think it happened and I'll spare you the details of how it really did."

She looked at him and pondered it a minute as they walked along. "I know, sorry." She looked down and dropped her chin in her hands. Her head bobbed with each step Ennon took. "Did it hurt?"

"Nah, there's no pain. It's like, well, like gatherin' water without the well. A little harder, but still manageable." He looked over at her and winked. "Make sense?"

"No, but your kind never has, so I'm not gonna go and try an' figure it out now. Should 'ave just done it like I said," she added slightly under her breath.

"No way, Aisling, that woman was married. As it stands, Pa's gonna be angry with me if he finds out what I did, I don't need to add the Maker on top of it. It just wouldn't be right, not like I would know a thing about it, anyways."

"You mean?" Aisling stood up again, swaying with his movement to keep her balance and placed her hands on her hips and let out a huge bellow. "Ennon R'yor, the village swee'heart… inexperienced? HA!"

"I'm glad I can cause you so much joy," he said and made a gesture as if he was going to flick her off of his shoulder, but she frowned at him in warning. "I wouldn't classify me as the village sweetheart, either," he continued and stopped her from a rebuttal on the subject. "I only had eyes for one lass and well, now that will never be." Tears welled up in his eyes thinking of the girl, Sebille, and hung his head.

"I didn' know, Ennon, I'm so sorry," Aisling offered and sat down, relinquishing any more teasing.

Ennon sucked in his lungs and shook his head subtly to wash the memory away and smiled. "I may not know love in my lifetime, but I will know what it's like to be a father," he joked, pulling Aisling out of her mood as well.

"From afar, if yer even that lucky," she joked back. "When all this settles, I'll make it me personal mission to find ye a mate, Ennon."

"Well, thanks, my friend, but I'm not too worried about it anymore. You didn't happen to bring a basket of food with ya, by any chance? I could eat a Minotaur right about now," he smiled, trying to lighten the now heaviness between them.

"Like I could carry one of those creatures on me back," she laughed. "Nah, I'm not that kind, remember?" she teased as she pulled a smaller parcel from her skirts and threw it towards the ground. As it fell, it morphed and twisted into a medium sized basket and landed perfectly on path in front of them.

"Has anyone ever told you just how amazing you really are, Aisling?" Ennon skipped ahead, grabbing the basket, which he discovered was heavy and found a spot under a tree, sitting down and laid the basket in front of him, opening it to find the feast that she had brought him. "Truly, truly amazing."

"Daily. Now, what I want to hear is how ye know it worked at all?" she said, landing on the corner of the basket, sitting down, letting her legs hang over the edge of the inside. She kicked at a grape that was sticking up towards the top.

"That's what took me so long. I wanted to make sure it took. Those humans could sure benefit with a little Fey magic," he laughed, "that's for sure. Takes forever for them to know things over there, it would drive me mad if I had to wait on things like that. I left the minute the woman declared her condition to her husband. Babe might even be here by now."

"Well, that's that then, isn't it? We just go about our business then?" she asked.

"For now, yes. I'll make sure to check on the babe from time to time to make sure it's well and safe. Maybe you can even help with that for me if you want?"

"Always passin' off the dirty work to me, ain't ya?" she teased, winking at him. Secretly, she loved having things like that to do, but it wasn't as much a secret to the ones that knew her, but it was an unspoken agreement to anyone who knew Aisling not to spoil her fun. Ennon looked at her while biting off a piece of the bread from the basket.

"Why don't you head back? I can make it back from here," he said, looking around. He knew the lands well and remembered the way back to the safe house. "It would make an awful long journey back for you, if you went the whole way with me. Besides, it would spare you my father's ranting, if nothing else."

"I dunno, Ennon. My orders are to see ye back safely in one piece."

"You say that as if you don't know my skill, Aisling."

"I know, I know, but if anythin' was to happen to ya, I would neva hear the end of it from Faolan, or yer family."

"Then I will be extra careful, I promise," he said and took a large swig of the ale that had also been a part of the feast. He wiped his mouth with his sleeve and rested his head back on the tree. She too would feel a great loss if anything happened to Ennon.

139

"It's gonna take some time getting used to, ya know, but I think in time things will get easier fer ya, now that you don't have a bunch of creatures to look after." Aisling joked, trying to convince both of them that it wasn't as bad as it really was, but it wasn't working and she suddenly wished she was bigger so that she could hug away the tears that were now streaming done both of their cheeks and settled on flying up and settling in the crook of his neck, where Ennon placed his hand on her gently and leaned into her, needing the same thing.

~~*~~

With the list in her hand, Hattie led Faineth to another spot in the forest, promising she would know why when they arrived. They had spent almost an hour planning before they set out to the Tower of Knowledge, as Hattie described it, and after hearing all that she had to say, Faineth was glad for it. Most of the things on the list, Faineth hadn't even thought of. She found herself grateful for the help and followed willingly.

"When we get there, dear, you'll mind to do exactly as I say, right?" Hattie directed as she walked along the forest floor faster than Faineth had anticipated. As small as she was, Hattie was quite agile and never once tripped on the debris bellow them. Faineth couldn't say the same, tripping often trying to keep up with her.

"Yes, I promise," she agreed.

"Now, then, it's just up ahead here," she continued and Faineth looked out past her small guide, but saw nothing but more trees.

"Use your senses, child. Those are clearer than mere sight."

Faineth didn't close her eyes, but concentrated more, instead. More on the things around them and the air in front of

140

them and like a mirage coming into full view, a large pillar of stone appeared in front of them about one hundred yards ahead. It almost stopped her dead in her tracks. She had never in all her young life seen a structure so massive that was made by hand. Her eyes followed it up to the sky, but it disappeared in the expanse of the forest, not revealing its true height, but the width suggested it could possibly lead to the Maker, himself. The stones which it was built from were almost green with all the moss and brackens that had grown on them and they were not all equal in size, but all seem to fit together in a way that she knew nothing, not even a dragon, could destroy it.

"Beautiful, isn't she?" Hattie asked. It wasn't quite the word that Faineth would have used, but it was very impressive so she simply agreed.

They continued until they reached the bottom of the tower and Faineth noticed a large wooden arched door, with vines growing over it, vines much like her mother's favorite and she felt a small pang in her heart at the sight of it.

"She will forgive you and she'll be happy you did what you did, so no sense worrying now, dear, we have much to do," Hattie said, reading Faineth's worry. Faineth was over being surprised at the many talents of Hattantia Peraladonus. She reached under her top skirt and pulled out what looked like a long, old, rusted key. Hattie kissed the tip, mumbled some words foreign to Faineth and simply tapped the key in the center of the door. What happened next caused Faineth to step back a few steps and smile.

The vines came alive and snaked along the door as if they were retracting from the place they once rested, but in a way that it looked as if they were snakes slithering along the grain of the wood. It was almost pretty to watch, really, and Faineth found herself wanting to touch them. She mindlessly stretched out her hand in front of her, only to receive a slap from Hattie.

"I wouldn't be doing that, lass, as pretty as they are they would soon kill you for trying. Those are deadly Thorn Lotus vines. One touch and you will wish you hadn't." Hattie placed her arm protectively in front of Faineth and waited till the vines had disappeared into the walls of the tower that surrounded the door. "Now, then," she said and took a step forward placing the key in the now visible lock to the left of the door. She turned it to the right, then turned it the left again, finishing with one last turn to the right, each time causing the old lock to click in agony, sounding as if it had wished to be left alone. Hattie placed her hand on the door and softly stroked it, humming as she did and Faineth swore she heard the door...purr.

"All it needs is a little love and it softens right up, see?" Hattie answered her unspoken question. "That's the way with all things, don't you think?" she had already gone inside and headed up a flight of stairs. Faineth followed and the minute her feet crossed the threshold, the door slammed tight behind her and she could hear the vines slithering back into place. Her body shuddered at the sound and she stepped closer to the stairwell, thinking that putting distance between her and the door was a good idea. She shook her head to clear it and looked up the stairs. They spiraled up unevenly as far as her eyes could see, with no sign of Hattie anywhere.

"Hattie?" she called out, feeling fear rise under her skin.

"Hurry up, dear, it will take the rest of the day to get to the top if you stand and gawk," came Hattie's voice from above and Faineth took off running up the stairs taking two or three at a time until she caught up with her. She was out of breath when she finally did and Hattie just sighed looking at her. "With a pace like that, you will never make it to the top, child. Slow and steady, I always say."

"Ya, you're probably right," she said finding it hard to breath and continued the long journey up the stairs that seemed to lead to nowhere.

17. Liberation

The morning's light had barely peeked through the small slits at the ceiling's edge of the dungeon. Roanus, who had found it hard to sleep, had finally drifted off and managed a few hours before the light hit his face and woke him from the dreamless nap. He opened his eyes long enough to remember where he was and then closed them again and gave way to a soft moan.

"Sleep well?" mocked Borlaug. He knew all too well how sleep felt like in the dungeons.

"Quite," Roanus answered sarcastically. "Excited for your big day?"

"Listen, Roanus, I was thinking while you slept," he shifted his weight and inched closer to Roanus, so that he could say what he had to say more privately. "You have shown me kindness."

Roanus laughed and lifted himself up from the dirty dungeon floor. "Kindness…how? I've done nothing for you except snore in your ear the past couple of hours. How is that showing kindness?"

"For starters, you have given me reason to walk out of this prison and feel like I'm important again. I know you can understand what that feels like, to be stripped of feeling important."

"Yes," was all that Roanus said in reply.

Borlaug pulled at the chains that were attached to his ankles and reached inside his tattered excuse for a shirt. Watching him, Roanus wondered how anything could be hidden inside of it with how ragged it was. He pulled out a small hook and laid out on the floor as flat as he could and reached for Roanus. Roanus watched with a smirk and giggled at the sight of him.

"I'm not doing this for your amusement. Come as close as you can to me with your back to me and you better make it quick, we haven't much time, stupid man!"

Roanus was too surprised by his request to get offended by his remark and did what he asked. He crawled as close as he could get then turned, laying back, but lifting his head up while Borlaug quickly attached the hook to the inside of the back of his collar.

"What on my mother's grave are you doing?" Roanus jerked back causing the hook to break loose and clank against one of the few stones on the floor.

"Shh, you fool! Quick, come back so that I can secure it again. You idiot, this is what's going to save your life!" Borlaug was becoming irritated by his cell mate's lack of trust.

"And just how is that hook going to save my life?" Roanus mocked.

"By not allowing the noose to break your worthless neck," he huffed.

Without further question, Roanus laid back down, holding as still as stone until Borlaug had secured the hook. He sat up and got back to his side just as the Royal Guard turned the corner at the end of the long hallway that led to their cell.

"This will allow you to complete your mission and make it to the safe house to finish off the family and all will no longer be in vain," he hurriedly said in a hushed tone so the approaching guards wouldn't hear him. The sparkle in Roanus' eyes told him that he had finally gotten to him. Roanus knew how hangings were conducted. After the prisoner fell through the scaffolding, the body was retrieved, but it took several minutes, even if there was only one hanging. The guards had other things to tend to right after, like keeping the mob of people that had come to watch from killing each other of differences of the hanging. They figured that the prisoner was already dead, so they could wait to be taken down. He looked up at Borlaug and smiled.

"Thank you, my friend, I will never forget this."

"You're welcome and to help matters, I'll make sure I celebrate my release openly," he answered and Roanus knew he meant he would help with the diversion that would buy Roanus even more time to escape.

"Just make sure your celebrations aren't too loud, Borlaug," mocked an approaching guard. "We don't want to see you in here again for being disorderly."

"Trust me, Peadar, seeing you anytime soon will not be counted as a pleasurable moment for me, either."

Peadar chuckled and walked over to the Changeling and bent down to unlock the shackles, which clicked loudly as the key turned. Borlaug grimaced as the thick bars that had been around his ankles for months gave way and fell to the ground. He instinctively reached for them, trying to rub out the pain they had caused with no success. He placed his hands on the ground and hoisted himself up and stood facing the guard. He looked up at him and smiled.

"Do I get a kiss goodbye, Peadar? Oh, how I will miss you," he jested.

"Leave before I disregard the orders and place your ankle jewelry back on, right after I cut out your tongue, so that I don't have to listen to you droning about anything again," Peadar answered sternly, staring down at Borlaug, without waver.

"Your loss," he said and shimmied his way around the guards, but not without turning back to look at Roanus and winking at him. He walked out of the cell and down the long hallway and just as he was about to turn the corner, he turned again. "It was a pleasure doing business with you," he called out to Roanus, but Peadar assumed he meant him and snickered.

"The King has allowed you breakfast before you are to be hanged and has said you may choose anything you want. Any requests?"

Roanus thought for a minute and smiled. "I'll take a steak, bone in, with bread pudding and I wish to eat it alone, if you don't mind," he answered.

"Not like I was inviting myself to join you. Tell the cook his order," he said to another guard standing behind him. "You'll have fifteen minutes to eat in peace and then it's the gallows for you." Peadar turned and walked out of the cell while the remaining guards followed, no doubt organizing the execution that would be taking place shortly. Roanus rubbed his temples, not out of pain, but out of nervousness. He had gone from despair to hope in a matter of minutes all because of the courtesy Borlaug had shown him. If he could make this work, then he could slip away, knowing all the secret passages in the kingdom and get to the safe house to perform his final revenge before disappearing forever into the wilderness.

~~*~~

The heavy odor of moss and mildew filled her nose as they climbed one step at a time. The air was so thick it was hard to even breathe, let alone smell and Faineth started to feel a little claustrophobic. The stench was leading her to believe that they hadn't been used in years.

"These do have an end to them, right?" Faineth felt as if she had been climbing stairs for half a day's time and every square inch of her body agreed.

"Everything worth having in life takes time and patience, my dear, but a bit of fairy magic doesn't hurt either," she said reaching under her top skirt and pulled out a small pouch. She reached a couple of fingers in and retrieved a small amount of dust and before Faineth could question her on what it was, she pointed them at her and blew the fine powder in her face. Faineth sneezed twice and blinked her eyes from the irritation but then noticed something remarkable. Her whole body, from the tips of her toes

146

ending at the top of her head felt relief. The muscle pain and ache was replaced with a new energy and she felt as if she could now run up the remaining stairs. She looked down at Hattie and giggled.

"Is there *really* nothing you aren't capable of?"

"Well, considering I haven't done all that's to be done in life then no, I'm not sure, but if I ever do, I will be sure to let you know. Now then, ready?" she turned and continued the climb once again, this time Faineth followed with a smile on her face and a bounce in her step.

It took about another hour of climbing to finally reach the top of the tower. The stairs led them to what appeared to be a lookout, large and circular, with sides high enough to feel safe from falling off, but low enough to see out as far as the eye could see. As soon as Faineth stepped out onto the flat stone, Hattie closed the hatch concealing the stairs.

"Don't want to be falling through that, too much to do today to be adding injuries to our list," she muttered and reached under her top skirt and pulled out the list. The wind had picked up with how high up they were, causing the parchment to rustle in her hands. "Oh, we can't go and lose that, now, can we?" She walked to the middle of the eye of the tower and started to turn around in circles until her skirts fanned out whispering the word "calm" over and over again. With every turn, the winds slowed until it was calm, just as she asked, then she came to a stop and smiled. "That's better."

Faineth laughed again, but Hattie seemed to ignore it and continue with the business at hand.

"What are we doing up here, anyways?" She had only then realized that Hattie had never told her what the climb to the top would bring them.

"Silly girl, haven't you been paying attention at all? Why, to see, of course," she said, slowly walking towards the edge and looking out over the lands below them.

"What are we trying to see?" Faineth asked, getting a little frustrated with the half riddles chatter she was getting out of Hattie. All she wanted to do was find Willow and get back to the safe house.

"Dragons."

Faineth turned and faced the wall of the tower, hopeful to see some sign of life. The view was actually spectacular. One could see all of Ethreal from where she stood. Looking out, she saw the peaks of the Castle Baelian and knew to look east to find the Liastreil Mountains, the former backdrop of what once was her village. She saw other things, peculiar things, and it made her realize how much she really didn't know of her world.

"What's that? Just there. See?" She pointed out to another tower, much smaller than the one she was standing on, yet proud enough to grab her attention.

"Well, that there would be the home of Lady Breaga. Surely, you've heard of her, now," asked Hattie in a semi-snide tone. "And if you haven't, best not to let her know that. She has an ego the size of a mountain. Best to always stay on her good side, I always say."

Faineth giggled. "Yes, I have heard of her, not necessarily the ego part, but she is a good friend to Queen Anya, right? My family knows the Royal family personally," she said with more shyness than arrogance.

Hattie picked up on it immediately and looked at her with affectionate eyes. "And that, dear child, is why you are standing here beside me with your heart still beating and eyes to see." Hattie walked over and stood beside Faineth, looking out in the same direction. "Tell me, what else do those eyes see?"

Faineth had already begun searching for the mountains again, but smiled down at Hattie remembering the kindness that had been shown to her and her family by the King and his. It gave her an instant feeling of connection to something other than her own family and the dragons she loved so dearly. As she looked out now, finally locating the mountains, the feeling of security was replaced with despair. For in all that she could see, dragons were not among them.

"Nothing," she answered bleakly.

"Nothing?" she asked again, looking back out in the directions of the mountains, with a puzzled look. Without turning to face Faineth again she asked another question. "Are your eyes open, child?"

Faineth giggled. "Yes, why would you ask that?"

This time she turned and faced Faineth before answering. "It's only that…" she turned back around towards the mountain range, obviously confused and seemingly, bordering on frustration. She looked back up at Faineth. "Do you really not see?"

Faineth furrowed her brows and shook her head. She looked back out towards the caves and shook her head again. "I'm not sure what you are seeing, Hattie, but there isn't any dragons in my view. I wish there were," she answered, her last words barely over a whisper.

Hattie rubbed her chin with her index finger, contemplating a thought. She smiled and laughed, startling Faineth.

"How far in your courses did you get, girl? Have you not learned the survival instincts of a dragon yet?"

"Survival instincts? Well…yes…some," she admitted.

"Well, that explains it, then. Melian must have seen a reason at the time to skip ahead I guess, but still…but then he wouldn't have foreseen a necessity for it I suppose, but it would have been handy right about now if he had…" she rambled.

"Hattie," Faineth cut in, interrupting her long winded debate, jolting Hattie's attentions back to her.

"Sorry. I guess I will be your teacher today, then. Right," she continued, composing herself better and taking a deep breath before explaining to Faineth about a dragon's will to live. "Have you ever asked yourself how some of the dragons aren't seen by others outside of your clans?"

Faineth thought about it for a minute and realized she really hadn't ever thought about it. She assumed that everyone within sight range could see if a dragon was near. Slowly conversations at gatherings and certain trickeries of the creatures played out in her mind and it all started to make sense. "They have the ability to *become* invisible, it's not just a spell…" she whispered, her words a statement more than a question.

"Yes, child, they do and all you need to do to see them is look with your heart as well as your eyes." Hattie smiled wide again at Faineth, who turned around back towards the mountains. She focused her eyes and strained, trying to "see" her beloved dragons but still found no sign of them. Frustrated she frowned and rubbed her eyes and tried to relax them, thinking they would come into view that way.

"Ugh! Still nothing!"

"You're trying too hard. Don't be forgetting who you are. You're a Guardian, child; it's in your nature. Now, then," she turned to face Faineth, grabbing her hands, forcing Faineth to look down and concentrate on her. "Try and empty your mind of any thoughts other than those of the dragons. Close your eyes and visualize them. Remember their flight patterns, their mannerisms, and when you have all of that, open your eyes…and see."

Faineth took a deep breath, letting her mind relax and started to think of Willow. She pictured her curled up on the edge of her bed, how her long tail swooped down across her mid-section when Willow would ride on her shoulders. She smiled as she remembered just how beautiful her wings were when she extended them fully; the transparency of the membrane and the opalescence of the scales. Willow was truly a sight to see, one she would never be fully contented with. She would never grow tired of the wonder of her beauty. She thought of the other dragons of her clan, as well, and felt a calming sense flow through her and she was once again reassured that Willow was still alive. With her eyes still closed and picturing the rest of the dragons from her clan, she relaxed her body with a soul cleansing sigh and smiled. She felt Hattie's hands squeeze around her.

"Now, open your eyes and see them," she said softly.

Faineth turned and slowly opened her eyes and the view in front of her now caused her to gasp. She saw them, flying and swooping in the skies, some more erratically then others, but the scene caused both joy and concern. Not only were there fewer dragons, but there were several she didn't recognize. She turned towards Hattie with confusion. Without having to ask, Hattie answered her brooding question.

"They have come for you, dear."

"What do you mean?" Faineth asked surprised and turned to see them again.

"Dragons are wise creatures, are they not? They know the devastation of what has happened. They also know that your family is all that remains. They have gathered together to be one herd…your herd, Faineth," she said warily. She wasn't really sure how Faineth would take learning she had just acquired what was left of the dragon species and by the looks of her, neither was Faineth.

She blinked hard and shook her head a little, trying to process what Hattie had just told her. It was a shock to see them, let alone take on the reality that she was their Guardian now. The severity of what Hattie had said hit Faineth hard, much like a club to the back of the head would feel; only this drove straight through her heart.

"One herd of dragons… mine?" she whispered confusedly and painfully and leaned against the tower wall to steady herself from collapsing. Everything that had happened in the last few days, all the things that she had seen, witnessed firsthand, came crashing back into reality, as if the surreal, self-preserving cloak that had been wrapped around her subconscious had been yanked away, violently, with that one truth spoken by her new friend.

"I can't…" she confessed, her voice full of fear. She turned towards Hattie and begged her with her eyes to admit this was all a dream and she would wake up soon.

"You must," Hattie answered, reaching out to Faineth, softly touching her arm.

"What now? How do I get to them safely? We're still so far away. It will take me days to get to them on my own." Faineth's words were filled with worry and she wished that Faolan was there to help her.

"Ah, but you won't be going just yet," Hattie told her and lifted her hand to silence Faineth's rebuttal. "You have things that need to be done first. Have you given any thought to where you all will be living now, dear?"

She looked back out towards the dragons and sighed. "To be honest, Hattie, I was just going to rescue Willow and return to the safe house."

"Well, that might work for some of the species, dearie, but you'll have your hands full with the others. You have close to fifty species, it appears, that need caves and three of those need to be underground if they are to feel at home."

Faineth took a deep breath thinking she had dragons to care for from the notorious Under Dwellers clan and decided it would be best to let the men in the family take care of those.

"Now, mind you, many feel all the Blacks were destroyed," Hattie added. "But don't give up just yet," she winked and Faineth wondered what she meant by it. "You still have plenty to learn…which brings us to your next task. Oh, but before we forget," she continued, fishing something out from under her skirts. She pulled out a rusted old ring that had several keys of all shapes and sizes, as well as what appeared to be a long thin whistle. "Here you are," she said to the noise maker and pulled it free of the ring, handing it to Faineth.

"What's this for?" she asked, holding the whistle in her hand. The closer she looked at it; an intricate design came into view. The whistle itself was much smaller in Faineth's hands than it appeared on Hattie's ring, making it harder to see at first. She lifted it closer to her eyes to get a better look and the design came to life. Two long, thin dragons intertwined themselves around the shaft of the whistle and Faineth would swear on her great grandfather's grave that they were moving. She smiled and looked up at Hattie and was about to say something, but when she looked back down, they had stopped.

"Why, to summon the dragons when we are ready for them, dear," she answered, pointing out back out to the mountains where Faineth could still see a few flying around.

"And they will *all* come when I use this?" She found it hard to understand how something so little could do such a task. "What about the ones still in the caves?" She didn't know how many were still down there, but one in particular had her concerned.

"The dragons have never been known to leave any of their kind behind, lass. I don't see them starting to any time soon. Now then, shall we get going?" Hattie turned on her heels and headed back in the direction of the stair case

"We came all the way up here just to see them?" Faineth asked, her frustrations once again, reaching a level that bordered anger, which Faineth didn't want to see happen, but at the same time, she couldn't understand all the steps she had to take just to get Willow back.

"The sooner you understand that this is much bigger than just you getting your pretty white dragon back, the sooner it will all start to make sense. Everything in life is a lesson, child. Some are good lessons and some are bad and some even test your very soul," she lectured, turning back around to face Faineth, pointing her finger at her when she said the word 'soul'. "But no matter, they are all vital. Always remember, dearie, you go nowhere by accident in this world. Every step along your journey has importance and one should never take those steps lightly, including these," she said as she started to descend down the spiraling stone stairs (that had taken them half a day to climb), disappearing from sight, but not from sound. "These here steps are steeper going down than they are coming up, so watch your step, please," she continued to talk but her voice was growing faint as she made her way back down to the bottom.

Faineth looked out across the horizon once more and squeezed the small whistle in her hand.

"Soon, Willow, hang on till then, okay?" she asked the wind and turned to join her small friend at the bottom.

18. What Evil This Way Comes....

The air was cold for this time of year and the clouds swirled in angry shades of muted gray above their heads as they approached the platform. A storm appeared to be brewing but the clouds would sometimes take on that form when death was coming.

"Fitting, but not today," Roanus chuckled. The guard behind him nudged him forward. He turned slightly, feeling the tug of the hook well hidden in the collar of his shirt and glared at the guard. "And did I commit this crime directly to you?"

The guard was taken aback by his inquisition but steadied himself quickly.

"These crimes you will die for today, *Hand of the King*," the guard answered, his words mocking when he spoke of his title, "affect us all."

Roanus only laughed an irritating laugh in reply and settled back on his thoughts of the plan he and Borlaug had devised. If he did die today and not fulfill his end of it, at least he would know that it was still over. With the child gone, there would still be no other way the Guardians and their way of life would flourish. Without mates for Ennon and Faineth, their race would die out, eventually.

"You mock your own demise" The guard asked, obviously reacting to his laughter.

"No, you small-minded elf! What I mock is your inability to see that my death does not end things. The crimes I've committed will be complete, soon enough, with or without me."

His words seemed to have passed right over the guard as he continued to push him forward, now climbing the stairs of the executioner's platform. The old wood creaked under his feet and he looked out over the courtyard, gazing upon the few faces that were there. His brother had promised him it would be a private execution, not an open to the masses, but he had obviously allowed a few watchers. He saw the guards that had been involved with him and his orders directly, scattered around the platform, not really together, but not far apart, either. As he looked at each of their faces, his heart grew colder, for in each one of their eyes he found no sadness, no pain, and no sense of losing someone they cared for. All he saw was justice.

Then his eyes fell upon hers and the world seemed to stop. Her once soft, green-blue eyes, full of love and wonder, were now dark pools of lipid blue. Her face was void of any emotion and it was as if he was staring at a perfected carving of his daughter.

"Miren," he called out. "Why have you come?"

"I needed to make sure," she answered him coldly.

"Make sure? You came to see your own father die? Do you hate me that much?" he asked as tears formed, causing his vision to blur.

"No, I did not come here to watch you die. I came only to make sure you were going to," she started to turn and walk out of the courtyard, just as the executioner lowered the rope around Roanus' neck, almost missing the hook, but turned back toward him. "And no, I don't hate you. Hate is an emotion and I carry none for you any longer."

She smiled as if a curse had been lifted from her soul and walked away. Roanus slowly closed his eyes and the tears that had been welling up, cut a path down his cheeks as the floor gave way under his feet.

~*~

When she finally reached the bottom of the stairs, Faineth saw Hattie sitting at the base of a large goat willow tree, snacking on something that smelled delicious, causing her stomach to rumble in reaction. She stepped over to her all too comfortable companion, hoping there was enough for her, as well. Hattie was resting on an old tattered blanket that was made out of pieced together bits of fabric in all different shades of purple and someone, long ago, had taken the time to hand stitch flowers in bright pinks and yellow threads, randomly around the edges. Faineth could tell by looking at it, that it had to have been quite lovely when it was newly done.

"This is very beautiful," she said, complimenting the workmanship, in case Hattie was the one that made it.

Hattie looked up at her strangely, "T'is only a hang on wheat rye dear, not sure it deserves that kind of compliment," she answered her, waving the hang, or what most would refer to as ham, sandwich a little in her hand.

Faineth laughed. "Not the sandwich, although that does look delicious," she said and sat down, resting near the basket filled with foods she hadn't noticed in Hattie's possession before. Shaking her head at yet another of Hattie's tricks, she decided against questioning on where it had come from.

"The blanket," she continued, averting her attention away from the food and back to the pretty quilt. "Did you make it?" She rubbed her hand across the material and enjoyed the softness of the worn fabric on her skin.

"Nah, that would be the workings of my mother. I never did care much for the thread and needle business," she answered, sounding a bit ruffled, like someone would if they were thrown off their thoughts, or it was just that her mouth was full. Faineth couldn't really tell which one for sure. "Here, dear," she continued, handing a sandwich wrapped in pink parchment to Faineth. "You look as if you could use one of these."

"Thank you," she said, grabbing it and eagerly taking a bite, but not before her stomach grumbled one more time. "That's really good, thank you," she mumbled, her mouth full of hang and rye. As she chewed, she figured it was best to get back to the task at hand instead of chit chatting about family heirlooms and sandwiches.

"So, we have located what remains of the dragons," Hattie answered her unspoken thought and Faineth just smiled in awe of her abilities. "Next, we need to get the tools that were left behind for you, just in case this sort of thing ever happened," Hattie said, raising her eyebrows in a 'aren't we glad they thought of it' sort of way.

"Tools?" Faineth questioned and gave her a funny look. "Am I supposed to build something?" Panic rose in her chest thinking that she would have to, but then she thought of Ennon and was even more thankful that he had made it through their ordeal. He was an amazing craftsman.

"Not in that sense, lassie. Tools come in all forms. These are the tools of knowledge," Hattie lectured and smiled wide and set what was left of her sandwich down as she got up off the blanket and walked around to the other side of the tree.

"Do I need to follow you?" Faineth called out, taking another bite of her lunch, hoping that it wasn't over so soon.

"No, dearie, just you sit back and enjoy that hang," Hattie answered, sounding farther away than just the other side of the tree. Faineth furrowed her brows in question, but continued to chew without moving. But after a few more bites, Faineth started hearing odd noises, like heavy things being tossed around and metal clinking as if someone was banging cooking pots together, yet it was very muffled as if those pots were in the bottom of a large thick sack. Faineth leaned back against the blanket and propped herself up on her elbows to try and get a look at Hattie and what she was up to. All she saw was the side view of Hattie, bent over, her skirts waving at the bottom with the motion of her arms, digging inside something Faineth couldn't see. "Ah, here we go,"

Hattie said, standing up and turning back in the direction of Faineth, carrying what appeared to be books.

Faineth looked up from her sandwich as Hattie approached her, dropping one of the books down beside her. She looked down and immediately tossed her sandwich in her lap, seeing the title.

"*Dragons: Species, Abilities and Attributes*," she read aloud and opened it up to the first pages. Beautifully illustrated examples of every type of dragon imaginable filled the pages, each one followed with a full description including the magic that went with that particular dragon. Faineth smiled down at the book, knowing exactly what kind of treasure this truly was. "Oh, Hattie..."

"Yes, dear, it's a good one to have, as well as this one," she answered, handing the other one to her, then picking out some fruit from the basket. "You'll be soon thankful you have these in your possession, especially that one," she continued, pointing to the one she had just handed her. Even though there were no markings on the outside of the book to tell what it was, Faineth knew who it belonged to.

"This was Lord Melian's," Faineth sighed, feeling heavy all of sudden, having lost someone so valuable. "I'm not sure I should..." she started to say, handing the book back to Hattie. She felt completely unworthy of having such a book.

"And you think he has much need of it now, do you? Faineth lass, you need that book to continue your lessons and besides, he's the one that left it for you," she answered, smiling.

"He left it for me?" she asked, realizing what that meant. "So he knew what was going to happen?"

"Yes, dearie, I suppose he did."

Faineth looked down at the large book that she had seen so many times in her mentor's hands and her vision blurred as the tears stung her eyes. Visions of him reading from it filled her mind. The way he leaned to the left when he thought something was important or the way his eyes squinted when he was trying to be serious, instead of laughing when a spell would go wrong. She remembered a time when he was having trouble keeping his glasses in the right position on his nose and when she asked him about it, knowing he really didn't need to wear them, he replied quietly 'it makes me look like a professor, instead of a jester" and then he winked and kicked his heels up. She would eternally miss his loving guidance and light hearted ways. She let out a heavy sigh and looked at Hattie, one of the tears falling down her cheek.

"I'm not sure I can, Hattie," she said, half choking on the words, trying desperately not to break.

"I don't think it's a matter of can or can't, lass, I think it's more a matter of will or won't."

Faineth took a deep breath again without looking away from Hattie. The woman's face was filled with sympathy for her, but it didn't seem to lighten the heaviness in her heart. She was right, Faineth knew that much. She could do it; it was just way more than she had ever expected. She'd always dreamed of being the best Dragon Guardian the clans had ever seen, she just didn't count on being one of the only ones. She knew her family was spared from the devastation brought on by Roanus' madness, but they, Ennon included, had never centered their lives around the dragons like Faineth did.

She looked back down at the book now resting in her lap. She started to remember all the times she had seen Lord Melian with it in his hands, or sitting next to him on a table, or even resting in a pouch as he climbed upon a dragon. She let herself sift through all the pages and noticed that almost every page contained handwritten notes from him on various things. Some were about things the book left out, others were on how certain experiments or lessons went, but one in particular caught Faineth's eye. It was on the page referring to the spell used for changing a Fey to a human or vice versa, called the Magus Novo spell, which literally translate into magical change.

"After many days of what I would consider basic training, one student in particular shows great skill and since it is accompanied by a large desire to learn, I truly feel this student will do great things," Faineth read out loud, wondering who he was referring to. "It is of no wonder to me of course, knowing her since she was a wee child and that she comes from a long line of great Guardians, but I still find myself taking some credit for it as I am filled with pride at how well and how far she has come. Most students of mine will not show the desire and passion Faineth shows now, until they are much older." Faineth gasped. "He was talking about me."

"Of course he was, child. Who else would he be talking about?"

She thought about it for a moment, recalling all the clan folk who were close to her age, give or take a few moons and could do no more than agree with what her teacher had written. Sure there plenty who cared for the dragons and such, but most went to their courses because they needed to, not because they wanted to and if given the choice, she knew most would have picked another activity. The fact that Lord Melian recognized this and actually wrote in his lessons book was a humbling experience for her. She continued to flip through the pages with a renewed sense of self-worth and saw many things she hadn't yet learned. The responsibility of it all crept back and she felt once again overwhelmed.

"I'm not sure I will be able to learn the rest let alone try and teach Ennon. Wait a minute. Come again? What did he mean by 'a long line of great Guardians'?" she half confessed, half asked. Hattie raised her hands in the air, in an act of frustration and cut her off from going any further with her thoughts.

"So much negativity! Are you sure you are the same Faineth that Melian talks about here in these pages? Or is this the new "woe is me" version, cause I dare say I liked the old you better," she rambled. "Don't you know where you come from, child? Have you been living in the caves with the creatures this whole time? You belong to a long line of powerful Guardians,

Faineth. Something your folks should have told you about, not sure why they didn't. I'm sure they have their reasons, but it's no difference now, mind you," Hattie reached across and took the book from Faineth and laid it on top of the other one beside her, then grabbed both hands, forcing her full attention.

"Now, you listen and you listen well. Allow my words to sink in, aye? No one said this would be easy, or fun, but what you have here, right now, is a calling. To ignore it would be foolish lassie."

"A calling?" Faineth asked, completely confused in what the old wood gnome meant.

"Yes, a calling. Make no excuses; there's a reason you survived this tragedy and a good one, at that. People are spared for reasons they can't always comprehend, but in time, if they are lucky, it plays out before them and their questions are answered." Hattie squeezed Faineth's hands tighter, demanding more attention. "The last thing you want to do is slap the Maker in the face with an "Oh, why me," and "I'm just a girl" attitude. You need to grasp the gift that has been given to you, step up as the brave and true Guardian that you are, and embrace it for all it's worth." She let out a chuckle and shook her head a bit causing Faineth to furrow her brows in question.

"Do you really think," Hattie continued, "that little of yourself? You are special, Faineth and it's about time you realized it."

Faineth sat there, soaking up what Hattie had said and wondered if the overwhelmed feeling was going to be a constant in her life from now on. Other feelings haunted her, as well. She thought it was funny and not in a ha-ha sort of way, but more like the un-easy, life-throws-many-stones-at-you way, that one could feel a sense of pride and guilt at the same time. Pride that her love and talents towards her Guardianship had not gone unnoticed, partly due to her lineage, and guilt that so many others had to die.

"I know what you are thinking and as long as you don't let it consume you, it's natural, but you must move on from it. You have a gift, child. There are reasons the lessons came easier, a reason the desire to be the best burns within you." Hattie pointed at her heart with that last statement. "This calling's been with you since you were born, lass. Heck, the Maker probably foresaw what was going to happen and made you just for this!" she giggled, thinking the possibility of her words. She stopped, looked deep into Faineth's eyes, causing her to shift a little uncomfortably and smiled. "And now it's time."

With that, Hattie gave her hands one last squeeze, clapped hers to her lap and stood up, gathering what remained of their meal and placing it back into the basket.

"It's time?" Faineth asked, a little startled at Hattie's quick pace and got up as well, stepping off the quilt, which Hattie made quick work of folding and after placing it atop the basket that was now almost too full to close completely and said some words that sounded gibberish to Faineth, tapped all sides with her pointer finger and Faineth watched as the basket folded in on itself until it was the size of a field mouse. Hattie bent over, clutching it in her hand and slipped it under her skirt, probably in one of the many hidden pockets, thought Faineth.

"You still have much to learn and many things to do, before we retrieve that dragon of yours," Hattie said, winking at her.

Faineth's heart pulled at the thoughts of Willow and wondered why they couldn't get her first and once again, as if Hattie could hear her thoughts, her hand shot up, stopping any future requests of that nature.

"She's safer where she is, for now," she explained.

Faineth shook her head at Hattie and smiled. "Hattie, do you have the gift of Mind Sight?" Hattie only looked up at Faineth in reply. She winked at her again and this time, her eyes danced with twinkle and mischief. She then turned, walking towards a path Faineth hadn't noticed before, without another word.

19. Dilemma

"You may enter," called out King Baelian, answering a rapid knock on the door of his Library. He was looking over old family sketches and at that given moment, he really didn't care who was at the door needing his attention. He just wanted everyone to go away for a while. He hadn't planned on going to the execution, but went regardless of Anya's warnings that it would be in his best interest if he stayed away. He had decided last minute to witness his brother's death without formality and had chosen to stand towards the back of the crowd in full disguise, but the sound of the trap door opening and his brother's final struggle was more than he could bear. It was hard to believe that in a few weeks' time, he had lost both of his brothers, one from haste and stupidity and the other by his own hand. He retreated before the death could be confirmed to his chambers, hoping to work through the various emotions that came alone, but that was now a short lived desire. The large wooden doors creaked with strain as the intruder pushed them open.

"My Lord, a word, if you please," begged Peadar, somewhat breathlessly.

Carrig sighed, tossed the canvases aside and sat back, realizing that even though he had executed his brother, business at hand would continue.

"What is it, Peadar, and if you please, make it quick. I would prefer to be left alone the remainder of the day."

"I understand, Milord, but this requires your immediate attention," Peadar petitioned, trying to stay with protocol, but also feeling the severity of what he needed to share.

Carrig looked up, hearing the urgency in his voice. "You shall have it then, Peadar. What is it that has you so out of breath?" He stood and walked around the large, ornately carved table that had been in their family for many generations and stood before Peadar.

"Forgive me, Milord; my words are jumbled in your presence." Peadar could feel his cheeks redden at the thought of what was to come with his news.

Carrig put his hands on his shoulders and gave a small squeeze.

"Peadar, you are my most loyal warrior. My family owes you more than we could ever pay for the services," Carrig took a breath and his shoulders relaxed a bit before continuing, "And friendship you have bestowed upon us. Whatever it is you have to tell me, it will be without any judgment."

"It's Roanus, my Lord. He is gone,"

"I know, I was there," Carrig sighed and turned around, walking back around the large table, once again sitting at the equally ornate chair. He mindlessly stared down at his callused hands. Even though his actions were justified by the laws of the land, he wondered if he would ever be able to truly be at peace with his brother's blood on his hands.

"No, my Lord, he is gone. When my men went to see to the body, it wasn't there."

"What?" Carrig looked up at him, his mouth somewhat open in disbelief. "How can a dead man just up and walk away?"

"Forgive me, My Lord, I have no idea. One minute he was hanging, a few of us…" Peadar cleared his throat, not really wanting to confess to his King that the majority of the men standing around were in a way celebrating the death of his brother. "A few of us were talking with our backs turned and when we went to deal with the situation…he was gone."

Carrig lowered his head, shaking it side to side. "That is not possible, I was there," he said in such a quiet tone that Peadar almost didn't hear him. "What kind of magic is this?"

"If I may speak freely, My Lord," Peadar asked, interrupting Carrig's thoughts.

166

"Yes, yes, of course," Carrig answered.

"There were a few of us that overheard things while Roanus was being held in the dungeon, My Lord, but no one thought anything of it at the time. Just words between…I beg for your pardon…two fools, but now…" Peadar's words faded into contemplation and his eyes got as big as saucers as he realized what was happening. "My Lord…I think I know what has happened."

"Please, Peadar; this is not the time to force me to question what you know…just say what you must say." Carrig's tone was quickly becoming impatient.

"We overheard them talking about a plan to, what was his exact words," Peadar questioned himself. "To finish what Roanus had started. Do you think that means…"

Carrig stared in disbelief. "Get Faolan and hurry."

Peadar nodded and left the room before Carrig could explain why.

20. Unexpected

The wind had picked up and both Faineth and Hattie's skirts were dancing with each breeze. They had been walking the better part of an hour without conversation and neither one of them seemed to mind. Faineth looked around at the scenery and wondered if she would ever grow tired of it. So much beauty she hadn't ever seen before. It was all she could do not to imagine herself a sponge.

"Almost there, dear," Hattie shouted back to her, breaking their long silence.

"Where is there?" Faineth shouted back.

"You'll soon see, deary, you shall soon see."

Faineth looked around Hattie to get a better look at the path ahead. For so long, it had been nothing but thick brush and huge overlaying trees, that it was hard to see anything in front of her beyond Hattie's wide backside and her large brimmed hat, that she had mysteriously pulled from the basket before shrinking it to fit in her skirts. Faineth had at first wondered why the need, but knew now if she had a mirror, her hair alone would answer that question. She could feel the twigs, leaves, and whatever else was stuck in it. She tried running her fingers through it earlier and accepted defeat right away. Nothing would be fixing her hair except a hot bath and a strong comb.

While Faineth was quietly cursing her hair's disorder, the narrow path that they had been traveling on came to a fork and Hattie stopped abruptly, almost causing Faineth to walk over the top of her. She looked up to what appeared to be a large stump with a sign nailed to it. Two arrows pointing in opposite directions were carved into the sign with two symbols atop each arrow.

Faineth couldn't recognize the symbols or see an end to either path and wondered if the next destination was still a ways off.

"What do those mean?" she asked Hattie, pointing up to the sign.

"That's the markings of the old language. It's not used much anymore, but those of us that have been around fer a while know it well enough. That one there goes to Merwick Bay," she explained, giving Faineth's heart a jump. Merwick Bay was half a day's ride by dragon, west of her village. It was a shady sort of village itself, known for its illegal trading and questionable residents, but knowing she would be that close to Willow, Faineth would risk the visit. "But that's not where we're headed. We are going that way," Hattie pointed to the alternate path and smiled. Faineth didn't return the gesture. Anything leading away from Willow was not going to get her approval. Hattie, noticing the grimace on Faineth's face, shook her head and giggled. "All in due time, lassie, all in due time; there's someone we need to see first."

"And I suppose this…person…lives down this way?" Faineth asked pointing to the other trail.

"You catch on quick fer a young one," Hattie joked. "Now, mind yer step; you'll soon think the trees have a will to grab at yer feet with the way the roots scoot across the path."

Hattie gathered her skirts and turned in the direction of the path and with a skip, started out on the next part of their everquizzical journey. After a bit, Faineth soon found herself grateful to Hattie's warnings about the tree roots. Most were high enough you would have to be blind not to see them, but there were a few, that if one wasn't paying attention, would soon grab your toe and drag you to the earth. It reminded Faineth of the game called "skip rock" that her friends and she would play between lessons when they were little. Children would line up in two lines and one would try and walk down the middle of the two lines, without stepping on the rocks that the two lines of children had just thrown down to make the path tricky to maneuver. After a few minutes of remembering, she soon turned the roots into the same game, jumping and spinning between each lump in the path. She lost track of time doing this and it wasn't until she ran into the back of Hattie, who had stopped without her noticing, that she realized it was a lot darker than when they had started down this path to a 'person' Hattie had yet to reveal.

"Where are we? And when did it get so dark outside?" she asked, looking around, trying to get her bearings.

"It's not that dark. Come on, let's get this over with," Hattie said and Faineth would swear she thought the older woman was nervous.

She followed her on the path that now started to slope upward and the once random roots, suddenly became stairs, winding up higher than Faineth could see.

"This isn't another one of your towers, is it?"

Hattie turned and smiled. "No, lassie, but you might wish it was by the time we get there."

Faineth frowned and continued to follow Hattie up the now very steep stairs. "What was it with these people and their stairs, anyway," she thought to herself. The sky above them was also grabbing her attention. Swirls of clouds in all shade of grey danced above them as if they were angry and she wondered if it was a storm coming.

"It's just that Breaga up to her old tricks," Hattie scoffed.

"Breaga, as in Lady Breaga?" Faineth asked. "As in friend of Queen Anya's, Lady Breaga?"

"Ah, so you have been listening. Yes, child, the one in the same, but do us all a favor and let me do most of the talking. She may be a friend to Queen Anya, but she isn't your friend yet and she isn't the kind you want as your enemy, either." Hattie gave her a look to further relay the importance of her message and Faineth succumbed and rolled her eyes in acceptance.

"Fine, I'll be good. Anything to sit down again and maybe have something to eat?" she added, but Hattie didn't answer her. The higher they climbed, the smaller the stairs became, until she could skip three or four with each step.

"It's all about tricks with this one, Faineth, mind your step, dear," Hattie told her and stopped at what appeared to be the end of the stairs. Faineth furrowed her brows in question and turned to look behind her. Surely the stairs were much higher than this? At the bottom they looked as if they could have gone on forever. Shaking her head, she joined Hattie at the top.

"It keeps out the less desirables, dear. She's not really the tea and biscuits kind of person you see; well, that's unless she is visiting you, then you best have your finest out," she added, then turned away from Faineth to walk along the now free of roots, fairly even path that led straight up to the door of an oddly shaped, smaller castle, that looked to be built on the very edge of a pointy cliff. It had one large turret towards the back and three smaller ones in varied sizes that gave it a crooked appearance. The stone in which it was made from was also random in size, color, and pattern, making it truly an odd sight to see, causing Faineth to giggle.

"My home amuses you, child?" called out a voice that reminded Faineth of lush moss; smooth, deeper than normal, and moist. The voice was very audible, but there wasn't anyone there.

"Oh, here we go," whispered Hattie sarcastically. "My Lady, forgive her. She's been through a tragedy beyond measure," Hattie continued, louder and more formal than before. Faineth looked at her funny, not having seen this side of Hattie yet.

"I know the tragedy you speak of, Hattantia," Lady Breaga answered, giving Hattie a reprimanding response. "I am very glad to see she has her sense of humor back. Her spirits must be up, that's good. She will need them. Come, you know how I *love* to wait," she continued, putting strong emphasis on the word love, letting Hattie and Faineth know that they needed to hurry along. The two scurried up to the door and as soon as they were standing directly in front of it, the large wooden, oval topped door opened on its own. Faineth noticed the detailed iron work on the front, encasing a large letter B in the middle. It was quite beautiful and actually looked somewhat out of place against the harshly worn, dark, thick planks of wood that made up the bulk of the door. The hinges were made from the same ornate metal and she wondered how something so delicate looking could hold up such a heavy door.

"Beautiful, isn't it? A dear friend from the North made those. He is very good with his hands," caressed the voice, now standing in front of her in the form of a woman. Faineth gasped, for she had never seen her open the door nor a more exotically beautiful person. Her skin was the color of raw honey and her hair was a black as the night sky with no stars, but shiny like polished silver. It hung down, almost touching the floor, enveloping her like a cloak. She had pointed ears that peaked out from under her hair and eyes the color of the sky after the first snow, pale, pale grey. She had a chiseled jaw and high cheek bones, but her face was soft and feminine. In all, she was stunning. Her shimmery dress that puddled on the floor around her feet was a deep shade of purple, which made her unusual eye color stand out even more, making them almost ghost like. Her lips were the darkest natural red that Faineth had ever seen, almost as dark as fresh blood. She could only imagine how she was gawking and Lady Breaga's smile let her know it must have been embarrassingly obvious.

"Why, child, you act as if though you have never laid eyes on an Elvin Witch before,' she purred. Faineth noticed that when she talked, it made her brain feel heavy and soft, much like Willow slept when she was newly hatched. She wondered if it was some kind of hypnotic trance and managed to only shake her head in reply.

"This one here hadn't met the end of her shoe until Roanus went berserk," Hattie cut in, startling Faineth, who had forgotten she was there for a brief moment. "I'll assume you know what to do, then," she added, pausing to wait for the nod from Lady Breaga that she was on board. "I have a mountain of sock darning I must attend to. Now, Faineth, you listen and do as she says. I'll be back in a few days to collect you and complete the rest of the what-nots on our list of to-dos." She then turned on her heels and walked out, the large door shutting itself behind her. Faineth stood there, stooped, wondering what had just happened.

"Oh, I thought she would never leave," Lady Breaga openly admitted to Faineth. ""Sorry, Faineth, *you* are allowed to enjoy her company. I, myself, would rather eat a wood rat," she said smiling, "Which reminds me, you must be hungry?"

"Yes…very much," Faineth choked out, hoping desperately that wood rat was not on the menu. For some reason, this woman made her nervous. Not in the bad sort of way, but in the I-hope-I'm-good-enough sort of way and it didn't help that she was still trying to process the fact that Hattie had left her alone with a stranger.

"Well, then, first thing is first. A nice hot meal in your belly always helps the brain work better. It does with mine, anyways." Lady Breaga disappeared through another door and by the time Faineth's brain felt normal, allowing her feet to catch up with her; she was alone in the room. Looking around, Faineth had an odd sense of familiarity. There was no way possible for her to have ever been here before, but she couldn't shake the strong bout of déjà-vu.

"Are you coming, child? I don't usually allow guests to dine in here," Lady Breaga said in a kind but stern voice, not that Faineth would have argued with her. With one last glance around the room, she noticed a painting on the far wall and froze.

"Is that…me?" she asked hesitantly.

The painting of three women hung on the wall surrounded by a dark, ornate frame that reminded her of the front door. One stood with cascading black hair, which Faineth recognized immediately as Lady Breaga, another standing next to her, had cascading waves of golden hair which Faineth recognized as Queen Anya and the third sat beside her in a chair. Flame red hair draped her shoulders and she could have sworn she was looking in a mirror.

"That would be my dear friend, Clairn," Breaga giggled. "But you do look an awful lot like your great grandmother, don't you?" she turned and looked at Faineth, studying her features closer. Lady Breaga stood uncomfortably close to Faineth and her gaze felt as if it was boring into her soul. Her brain felt that hazy, dream state again and she wondered if this was one of the witch's tricks on how to read people. She instinctively broke the trance and rubbed her forehead.

"You're not the first to say that," Faineth said mindlessly. Lady Breaga's words started to sink in a little and she slowly turned around. "You knew my Great Gran? But, you look the same in the picture," she said leaning to the side to look at the painting on the wall that now hung directly behind Lady Breaga.

"I knew her well. She and I were sisters."

Faineth coughed on the large lump of surprise now lodge in her throat. "You were what?"

"Well, not sisters in the blood sense, mind you," she answered, turning and motioning with her hand for Faineth to follow as she continued her explanation. "Sisters in our coven… Clairn and I sat on the Council," Breaga turned halfway down a long hallway she had been leading Faineth through and looked at her again with piercing intent. "You know, there's a lot more about you that reminds me of your *Great Gran*, as you like to call her, than just your looks. Tell me, Faineth; were you top of your courses? Did blood magic come easy? Have you turned anyone …successfully?"

Faineth just stared at her. "Yes…to all of it," she squeaked out her answer.

"Just as I thought. Now, come with me. We have much to discuss, but it will have to be done over a hot meal. I truly am hungry and you are starting to look delicious and eating you is not on today's agenda."

Faineth felt the flesh bumps raise high on her skin and a shiver that started at her lower back, crawled up her spine at such a pace that it almost buckled her knees. How she actually started to walk behind her, following her to who knew where, was a shear miracle. She would have Hattie's head for leaving her alone with this witch, if she lived that long.

~*~

His boots echoed against the stone walls, as Faolan hurried to see his father. Peadar was beyond upset when he had come to tell him of his father's wishes to see him, so much so that Faolan couldn't grasp what the soldier's words meant, let alone understand half of what he was trying to say. Whatever that had caused him to be so flustered and the urgency behind his father needing to see him right away couldn't be good. He didn't bother with a knock and burst through the doors unannounced.

"Father?" he questioned, looking at Carrig, who was obviously distraught.

"Faolan! Thank you for coming so quickly. It is not over yet, son, and I need your help now. Please get your affairs in order, you need to leave within the hour," Carrig addressed Faolan without breaking for air. The immediate nature was evident in his voice, as he turned to face the large fireplace.

"Anything, Father, I am at your disposal." Faolan thought quickly if there was anything that would stop him from being ready, but couldn't think of any. "I have nothing of importance. What, if I may ask, is not over?"

"Your uncle's…wickedness. He has somehow managed to escape death," Carrig confessed, then turned looking Faolan in the eyes. His were full of pain and question.

"Roanus is still alive? How?"

"The details aren't known yet, but I believe I have figured out why and who might have helped him. I also have another theory I wish to discuss with you and it is the reason of your

175

departure. I just can't assume he wouldn't try something...,"
Carrig rambled, rummaging through the parchments arranged
haphazardly on the large table before him, but his son stopped him,
lifting his hand in the air.

"I don't need details of the why, Father. Just tell me what
you need me to do and it is already done," Faolan reassured him,
closing the gap between them and resting his hands on his Father's
shoulders. Carrig relaxed a bit at his touch and looked thankfully
into his son's eyes.

"The Maker blessed me when he gave me you," Carrig
admitted.

"He knew what he was doing," Faolan winked, then he and
father walked around to where two chairs sat facing each other,
bowed heads, and forged a plan that would hopefully put a stop to
his brother's twisted idea of justice.

20. Unexpected

Ennon left Aisling at the edge of the field and headed in the direction of the safe house. The sun was hanging in the sky, alerting him that he only had a few hours of light left and he was grateful to be as close as he was. He hadn't quite reached edge of the protection spell yet and found himself looking over his shoulder frequently because of it. Laughing at himself, he began to pick up the pace.

"Don't be fool-headed, Ennon," he giggled. The sky above, still empty, brought back some of the sadness he had spent the past week struggling to shake off. It wasn't that the devastation his family had faced was something he could brush under a rug, but he had too much to be thankful for to slap it in the face with all-consuming depression that hung in the background of his mind. He had accomplished so much and was truly happy to share it with his family, his most blessed, most fortunate Guardian family. He smiled at his last thought, knowing he had done what he must to ensure that very existence. Sure, the blood lines would be weakened at first, but with patience and blessings, that too would correct itself...in time. If only the dragon's had survived.

He looked ahead and saw the smoke from the safe house rise to meet the clouds and his smile widened. He couldn't remember a time he had been more excited with being home and he knew then, that wherever that was now, as long as his family was there, it would be home. In thought and half running, he also realized something else. When he had left to cross over, he remembered feeling the shift in air as he passed over the protection spell. He looked around wondering if he was farther back than he had first thought, not having felt it yet.

"I could have sworn...," he said out loud as he back tracked a bit, to where he was sure the invisible barrier rested and still felt nothing. "That's odd," he continued, looking back in the direction of the safe house. A feeling of something being 'off' washed over him and he took off towards it, running full on, praying he was wrong. It felt like it took twice as long to reach the door and when he finally did, he didn't hesitate to push it open. He stood in the entrance to what seemed like an empty house and started to panic. A movement in the shadows of the back of the house caught his eye.

"Father?"

A bruised Arien walked out into the dappled sunlight, struggling to talk. Ribs broken, he took a ragged breath.

"Ennon…my son."

"Father! What has happened to you? Where is Mother?" Ennon took a hurried step in the direction towards Arien as he looked around the room for signs of his mother.

"Ennon, no… stay there, son…please," his father gasped, obviously struggling to talk without pain. Ennon's blood boiled and wondered where the rest of his family was and what their fate had been if his father looked like this. Arien was a strong man, not one to lose a battle by any means, so to Ennon, if he looked like this, then what…

"Faineth?" he questioned, fear gripping him as he took yet another step towards his father. Arien's hand shot out faster than he thought possible and he grimaced with the pain it caused.

"She's not here. She left a few nights ago. You must leave here now and find her, Ennon," his father struggled and Ennon saw a tear streak the cheek of the man before him. A man he would have sworn was not capable of such emotion. "Please, son, she needs you now."

"What do you mean *she* needs me now? You look as if you could use my help more, Father. Please tell me what happened and where is Mother?" he went to call out to his mother when he heard another sound of pain from his father, as if someone had just hit him from behind.

"Father?" Ennon questioned then gasped as the tip of a blade protruded out from his father's chest. "Father!" Ennon went to grab his father as he fell to his knees, but stopped and looked in the face of the man who had caused his father's suffering.

"Ah, we finally meet. I was hoping it could be under different circumstances, but alas, since you have such a strong mind of your own, I felt it… necessary…to handle things… personally."

"Who are you?" Ennon's rage was filling his soul faster than his logical brain could keep up. He wanted to finish this man before him and ask questions later, but he knew if he killed him now, he would never learn the whereabouts of his mother or Faineth.

"Seriously, boy, and here I thought the R'yor's were friends of the Royal family," the man mocked. "Don't you recognize the Hand to the King?"

"Roanus." Ennon half whispered, fear settling on his heart like a surprise autumn frost. "Where's my mother? What have you done with her?"

"Ah, yes. Olorin actually put up more of a fight then old Arien did. It's quite amazing the strength and raw determination of a woman in danger. What she won't do to save her family," Roanus spoke as if he was in wonder at witnessing Olorin's struggles and glanced away briefly. Ennon went to take a step in his direction when something out of the corner of his eye caught his attention. He went to turn to look at it and felt the blow of Roanus' hand to the side of his head and blackness over took him. The last thing he felt was his body hitting the floor.

21. Weakness and Strength

Despite Faineth's apprehensions, the meal Lady Breaga provided for her was quite good and neither of them spoke until their bellies were full. They sat together in a large library of sorts, at the end of the kitchen area. The sorts part was due to the fact that the books were stacked in large piles all over the room, stacks that threatened to fall over at any minute and Faineth couldn't help wonder if magic was holding them up. Finishing first, Lady Breaga watched with a smile and marveled in the likeness that her little visitor held to that of a friend lost long ago.

"Tell me, Faineth. How much has your mother spoken of your great-grandmother Clairn?" she asked, propping her elbows on the table and relaxing on her chin on her folded hands.

"Not much, just that I looked like her," she answered, chasing the last potato around the bowl with her fork.

"Look like her? Ha! You are the spitting image of her, child! When you first stepped on my path, I thought it was her, coming to visit," she half laughed, half sounding relieved. "I've never been one to entertain ghosts before, spirits maybe, ghosts, never. They always want you to solve their issues so that they may pass over. Dirty business really, gave it up years ago actually. Quite time consuming," she rambled on, drifting off in a deeper thought.

"Exactly like her?" Faineth asked, feeling slightly at odds about it, but not as spooked as the whole idea of ghosts visiting had.

Lady Breaga leaned forward, staring in that *directly into her soul* way again, causing her to look down at the now mangled piece of potato in her bowl, which didn't help. She still felt her gaze on the top of her head.

"Yes and I'm not sure whether to be spooked or amazed, really," she answered without removing her stare. "I wonder…"

Faineth looked up and watched Lady Breaga get up from the table and cross the room, where she began to rummage through one of the stacks of books that didn't appear to be in any order. Lady Breaga fished one out from the middle of one of the bigger stacks and brushed off the collected dust with her hands, then looked over at Faineth and smiled a smile that gave Faineth flesh bumps. She turned and walked back over to the table while caressing the book. She sat once again, this time next to Faineth, and started to flip through the pages. Faineth noticed that it was a type of journal but also had strange pictures on separate parchments within the book, stuck between pages. It was like looking at a mirror image of an object or person but on shiny parchment and found herself wishing she could meet the artist. Lady Breaga laughed.

"These aren't from an artist, Faineth. These are called photographs. Here, look," she said, lifting one of the photographs out of the book and holding it at an angle so Faineth could get a good look. Her eyes grew almost as large as her soup bowl.

"Is that her?" she asked, sheepishly.

"It's like you are looking back at yourself, no?" Breaga smiled and handed the picture to Faineth. "Here, this one is yours."

Faineth took the photo in both hands and studied it closely. The picture staring back at her was of a young woman, about the same age as Faineth was now and the only reason Faineth knew she was looking at an image of another person, and not of herself, was that she had never worn a dress like the one the young woman was wearing and she didn't recognize the background. Otherwise, there was no difference between them. The girl staring back at her had the same wild, flame red hair, the same cat-like eyes, same pointy nose, and exactly the same mischievous smile and she had been friends with Lady Breaga and the Queen, which would explain the family friendship.

"And I would bet you have the same abilities as your great grandmother. Something we will most definitely be finding out soon enough. Are you finished, then?" Lady Breaga didn't wait for Faineth to answer and took her bowl and walked over to the sink and dropped it in. She said a few words and the bowl spun around a few times and then shot over across the room, landing neatly at the top of a stack of bowls already sitting on the shelf.

"Cleaning dishes is such a bore. No wonder I don't do them often," Breaga rambled. She looked out the window and frowned. "We are losing daylight, little one. Let's get started before I change my mind. A warm bath is starting to sound more enticing than tutoring a young witch to greatness."

Faineth tucked her new treasure into her pockets and followed the older woman out of kitchen, hopeful that she could live up to Lady Breaga's and her grandmother's expectations.

~*~

Hours had passed and the darkness of night had fallen over the field which sprawled out behind the strangely shaped castle that belonged to Lady Breaga. She had shown Faineth countless spells and conjures that Faineth had accomplished masterfully without effort, much to Faineth's surprise.

"I wish Melian had survived. I would ask him what he was thinking by holding you back. Are you sure you have never practiced these spells before, Faineth? Do tell the truth, dear, I will know if you are not," she added, giving Faineth another uncomfortable feeling, like you would get if your teacher caught you messing around in your lessons.

"No, Milady, this is the first time I have done any of these. Most of them I haven't even heard of before," Faineth spoke up quickly, not wanting to be reprimanded for any reason.

"Interesting, you almost come across as bored, though, like you have done this before, or you aren't interested in what I have to teach you. Is this true?" Breaga asked with a slight edge to her tone and Faineth secretly cursed Hattie once again for leaving her alone with here.

"No. Lady Breaga, not at all! It's just…"

"Just what. child? I will not waste my time on someone who doesn't want to learn!" she half shouted in Faineth's direction, causing her to jump.

"As much as love learning all of this," she waved her hand around as if the lessons were objects around them. "I just wish I could have…"

"What?! Could have what?" Breaga interrupted once again. "Spit it out. child. I am not known for my patience!"

Now she was yelling, making Faineth even more jumpy and she took a few steps back, just in case what she said next got her a knock in the shoulder or worse.

"The whole reason I left in the first place was to find Willow! Not travel the countryside with Hattie, visiting and furthering my skills! I just want to find Willow," she said, letting her words trail after each other like a defeated army. She stopped caring what Lady Breaga would do with her. She missed Willow more than words could say and although she had kept her feelings of sorrow and emptiness about Willow at bay, it was no longer an option.

"That's what's keeping your mind off your lessons? By the Maker, why didn't you just say that to begin with? I could have saved us…*me,* so much trouble!" Breaga complained, shaking her head, then took a few steps back as well, creating an even bigger gap between her and Faineth. She lifted her hands in the air and looked up to the sky, but closed her eyes.

"Ameinia Protalus Demu Sevectim," she hummed and the skies grew darker than they already were, making it hard for

Faineth to see her. She turned her head in the direction behind them, swearing she heard a sound, but gave up with not being able to see anything around them. It was as if Breaga had created a void and they both were stuck in it. As the sound grew louder, Faineth grew more and more uncomfortable and sank down to her knees, fighting the urge to curl up into a ball. The sound grew louder and louder, yet she still couldn't make out what was happening. Closing her eyes as tightly as she could, she sunk down, waiting for the worst. Just when it was almost too loud to endure, the sound was gone and a bright light, brighter than anything that Faineth had ever seen before, surrounded them and she once again covered her eyes.

"There, that should help things a bit," Lady Breaga spoke, but it wasn't directed at Faineth, who was still too frightened to look up. She peeked out between her fingers at the ground and realized it was back to being the normal darkness of the time of night it was and slowly lifted up, still not looking in the Lady's direction. She relaxed her shoulders a bit then finally looked up at Breaga and gasped, almost choking. In Lady Breaga's arms was a beautiful small white dragon. Willow.

"Willow!" Faineth shouted, stumbling to get up as fast as she could, almost tripping on her own foot. The dragon, too, was half clawing her way out of Lady Breaga's arms and not wanting any pain, the woman dropped her. The two met in the middle of where they had been standing and Faineth almost crushed Willow in her arms.

"Oh, Willow! You're safe! You're alive! You're here? How?" she asked, looking back over to Lady Breaga, who was dusting off her clothes as if Willow was the dirtiest thing that she had ever carried.

"It's a simple retrieval spell. You could have done it at any time if you had known how to," she answered nonchalantly, as if what had just happened was no big thing. She looked at Faineth and tilted her head. "Really, child, all you had to do was ask. I could have retrieved her hours ago."

Faineth nuzzled her nose into Willow's neck as the dragon curled around her shoulders, searching out her 'resting place' that had been hers since she was hatched. Letting go and letting her settle in, Faineth took a step towards Breaga and smiled.

"Thank you, Lady Breaga. Thank you for everything, but now that I have Willow back," she said looking at her dragon and smiling. "We can go home."

"You will do no such thing!" Lady Breaga shouted and Willow dug into Faineth's shoulders causing her to grimace with the pain. "You, dear one, need to finish your lessons. You leave now and you might as well write your own death notice. Now, enough of that silliness; Willow can stay here if you promise you can pay attention and learn. We only have a few days before that do-gooder returns and I will not give her anything to mock me with. Am I understood?" she looked at Faineth with that soul piercing stare and there was no way she was going to argue.

"Fully," she answered, turning towards Willow again. "Okay, little one. I need to do this, okay?" she sighed and rested her head against her back. "I'm so thankful you are here," she added and felt her eyes get warm, signaling tears were on their way. She shook her head a bit and helped Willow down, placing her in the grass beside her. "Watch this."

Faineth raised her arms and spoke the words of one of the first spells Lady Breaga had taught her that afternoon. The air around them began to move and fallen leaves from the field picked up and started to dance around them. Faineth watched as Willow straightened up and craned her neck to try and catch one of them with her teeth, biting down without success. After a few attempts, she became frustrated and blew fire into the air, torching the leaves that danced in front of her. Lady Breaga smiled, walking up to stand beside Faineth and spoke a few words of her own, causing the fire to take shape and Faineth giggled at the sight of an exact replica of Hattie carved in flames. She was shaking her fingers at the two and Faineth looked up at Lady Breaga who was nodding at Faineth, her left brow arched in a this-is-what-we-can-expect sort

185

of way, causing Faineth to laugh out loud. She turned and wrapped her arms around Lady Breaga and held tight.

"Thank you for bringing her back to me," she whispered and Lady Breaga folded her arms around her, softly stroking the back of Faineth's head. She laid her head on top of Faineth's and smiled.

"You are very welcome. Now, I think we have actually had enough for one night. Tomorrow is a new day and it will be helpful to have the sun's help. Why don't we head back, see if Willow is hungry, and get some sleep?" Faineth looked up into the now soft eyes of Lady Breaga and knew instantly this is the version she liked the most.

"Sounds great," she answered, turning back towards Willow, but keeping one hand around Lady Breaga's waist and motioned for her to follow. The dragon lifted into the sky, completed two rolls and closed the gap between them, hovering above their heads, causing Lady Breaga to laugh.

"I can see why you are so attached to this one. She's quite entertaining."

The three of them turned and walked back in the direction of Breaga's castle, each one with a new sense of happiness.

Three days passed faster than Faineth could have imagined. Each day was so full of lessons, exercises, and discoveries that Faineth had to fight to retain it all. Each day also brought on sheer exhaustion, both mentally and physically, and today was the hardest so far to wake up. It was as if her eyelids had refused to cooperate because her eyelashes were weighted down. She rolled over in the lavish bed that was in the over-sized room that Lady Breaga had so graciously set her up in and let out a comfortable sigh. As much as her heart wanted to return to her family, it was going to be very hard to leave this lifestyle and return to the life of a Guardian. Sleeping on feed sacks and handmade blankets would never compare to the lushness of this bed.

Willow crawled up to greet her from the foot of the bed, stretching and sighing in the same way as Faineth had done and sprawled out beside her, laying her head down so that her nose touched the tip of Faineth's nose. The soft cat-like purring that Faineth had missed so much filled the room and she smiled.

"I missed you so much. I think it would be better if from now on, you and I stick together," she suggested. Willow, as if in agreement, nodded and snuggled in closer, folding her wings tightly against her back. Faineth wrapped her arms around the dragon and felt her back and wings carefully looking for any residual effects of injuries she might have gotten during the attack. "You seemed to have healed up quite nicely."

Willow grunted softly as if answering her question, then lifted her chin in a proud gesture to confirm she had indeed done just that. She pulled her wings free of Faineth's embrace and stretched them out as wide as they would go, so that Faineth could examine them closer. She noticed a small jagged line that stretched up almost the full width of her left wing and Faineth frowned at the sight of it.

"Did it tear?" she asked, looking back up towards Willow. The dragon, which Faineth seemed to think grew in size overnight, shook her head and lifted her chin, sending out a small, streamline beam of fire, stopping it before it could reach anything in the room. "Another dragon did this?" Faineth asked again, her frown growing into a scowl.

Willow nodded, but before Faineth could erupt in anger at the thought of a betrayal like that from another dragon, the door to the bedroom opened and Lady Breaga entered. She crossed the room and sat on the edge of the bed and Willow nodded at her in welcome.

"Good morning to you as well, Willow. I hope you and Faineth slept well?"

"We did, thanks," Faineth answered, still caught up in the idea that another dragon would hurt Willow.

Lady Breaga eyes stayed on Willow and her facial expressions changing ever so slightly. "She wants me to tell you it was an accident. She can feel you think it was purposely done and won't leave my thoughts until I clear the matter up," Lady Breaga stated in her typical non-expressive manner that Faineth was oddly getting used to.

"You can hear her thoughts?" Faineth asked completely caught off guard. She had heard tales of peoples who had the gift, but had never met anyone until now who possessed it.

"More than that, Faineth, I can communicate with her," she bragged.

Faineth looked at her with a mixture of shock and jealousy. "Teach me?"

"In time, in time, but for now, you need to concentrate on becoming the power you were meant to be. You can't expect to ride a horse without first earning its trust." Breaga smiled and stroked her arm.

"What's a horse?" Faineth looked at her puzzled and thought that despite the entire act, Lady Breaga was just crazy, but good at covering it up.

"Further proving we have much to go over before Hattantia returns," she said and patted her arm before standing up. "Get yourself cleaned up and dressed and we will have breakfast together. Maybe if we hurry we can get some more training in and I can introduce you to a horse." Lady Breaga then turned and walked out of Faineth's temporary bedroom, closing the door quietly behind her. Faineth just shook her head and looked at Willow.

"I'm going to do whatever it takes to be able to talk with you. Just think about how grand that will be, Willow! I wonder if we can talk even if we aren't next to each other. Wouldn't that be something?"

Willow nudged her chin then jumped off the bed and walked over to the basin that had a pitcher of warm water sitting next to it with a couple of towels and Faineth wondered when that showed up.

"I wonder if I'll ever be like her. She's not all that bad, really. Not like Hattie made her out to be, anyways," she sighed in answer to the tilt of Willow's head. "Maybe she is just misunderstood like we are," she continued, but Willow had other plans. Willow nudged the bowl, then looking back at Faineth, giving her a low growl. "Alright, alright, I'm getting up. So bossy this morning," she added with a smile. "You must be hungry."

Willow let out a soft bellow and before she could follow it with a flame, Faineth jumped down off the bed and went to get cleaned up.

22. Protection

The night air was colder than he had expected and the dampness was soaking through the soles of his shoes, but nothing was going to slow him down; he just hoped he wasn't too late. It had been ages since he had crossed over and he was secretly cursing Ennon for choosing this particular location. After all, he could have picked some place closer and possibly drier. Traveling undetected was easy with certain glamours, but the dampness can sometimes cause them to waver and the last thing Faolan wanted was to be seen.

When one from the Fey realm crossed over and is seen by someone from the human realm, it causes all kinds of problems. Depending on the location of the sighting, it could take days to get the proper help to "erase" the human's memory and restraining a human till that help arrives isn't always…fun. Most of the Fey that chose to come across used enchantments and humans would mistake what they saw as a dream, but some Fey were reckless and it was in those times that the memory wipe was needed. Luckily for Faolan, it was late enough; most people were in bed already asleep and he didn't need the enchantments. Unfortunately, because of the size of his wings, he did need a pretty strong glamour and if the rain didn't let up soon, he would lose it and have to fly high enough to make up for loss of having one and might cost him more time. He wasn't sure what would be waiting for him when he got there. His father's instructions were solid, but he wasn't sure if he would beat the Changeling to the location, or if it would be waiting for him. The idea of being too late was not an option, but he was prepared to fight, if he had to, and win.

Judging by the location of the moon, it had to be somewhere around two in the morning, human time. Peadar had told Carrig that the order had been sent sometime the morning of Roanus' execution, giving them all hesitation as to whether it would be a moot point trying to stop something that had already taken place. It was Faolan who convinced them they should at least try, knowing that not all creatures from their realm could easily

190

maneuver the human realm. He left without even trying to get word to Faineth and Ennon.

An owl's call came from above, giving Faolan a bad feeling that his glamour was failing and without taking any chances, he spread his massive wings and took flight. This part of the world had one wonderful thing going for it, he thought. It was lush and green and if he wasn't in such a hurry to get to his destination, he would enjoy the view very much. The moon shone through the parted clouds and he immediately got his bearings. He banked left and followed the rural road until it came to a small bridge that allowed a small creek passage, which meandered through the fields and knew the house wasn't much farther.

Occasionally, he would spot a vehicle and drop behind one of the many stone walls that surrounded the farmlands here, but it was so rare that one would pass; it didn't seem to slow him up. He could tell he was getting close when he saw a large field, where a flock of sheep, deep in sleep, nestled among the edge of a small gathering of trees. The silhouette of a large farmhouse came into view at the opposite edge of the field and he knew instantly with the description and directions he was given, it was the house he needed to find. Half rotted pumpkins with silly faces carved on the side littered the front porch and he laughed with mock humor. It would never make sense to him why humans felt the need to commercialize certain rituals and slap them on holidays that had nothing to do with their species.

He looked around cautiously before descending closer to the back side of the house, when a movement caught his eye. He landed around the other side, so that he could use the element of surprise to his benefit if it was the Changeling he was sent to stop.

"There you are, little one," a voice Faolan instantly recognized spoke. "It won't be long now and all the trouble you would have caused will be no more. Now to just get this open..."

"Not sure that is such a good idea, Borlaug," Faolan added before the Changeling could open the window to the infant's room.

The creature jumped at Faolan's voice and took a few steps back to collect himself.

"Ah, Faolan, what brings you here?" Borlaug's guttural voice was raspy from being startled as if he hadn't quite caught his breath. He looked at Faolan closely after the elf didn't answer him immediately and his brow pinched in concern. "How did you know?"

"Let's just say my father's prison walls have ears," Faolan answered hotly, his anger growing by the second. "The question is, what are you doing here, creature? Don't you have swamps to stink up?"

Borlaug laughed, but it wasn't a ha-ha funny sort of laugh, it had far too much sinister tone to it for that. "I would have assumed that was your expertise, Faolan, and my business is none of your concern." He turned, looking back towards the window as if he had just dismissed Faolan.

"If by your business, you mean to cause harm to that child, then yes, it is very much my business. I know what you and Roanus are up to and it stops here," Faolan stated, stepping closer to Borlaug, trying to wedge himself in between the creature and the child's window. At almost the same time, Borlaug took another step, making it hard for Faolan to get in between the two.

"You will not win this, Faolan. As we speak, the final preparations are being laid and as soon as you move aside, my work will also be complete, ending it all."

"Ending what all? You are making little sense with your words and if you wish to live through tonight, you will step aside and share what other plan is being played out," Faolan demanded. He could feel the burn of his wings in anger and lowered his hand to his side, the side that had the dagger if things were to get out of control and as far as he was concerned, it was headed in that direction.

"Well, considering it's probably already complete, I don't see any problems sharing that information with you," he gloated.

He shifted his body to be more face-to-face with Faolan and squared his shoulders, without moving away from the window. Faolan knew this was the creature's one weakness. Changelings loved to boast about their wicked ways and he was going to egg him on with this knowledge to get him to spill all he knew.

"You see, Faolan, for centuries, you and your family's...regard...has been shifting. Your father's complacency is going to be the downfall of your people."

"My father's complacency? Are you really that mad?"

"Mad isn't the word I would use, young elf. Educated is more appropriate. You really think that this kingdom values your family and its beliefs and the ways you have ruled this land? You think, because of the submissive nature so many show, that it really means that they blindly follow you? No questions asked?" Borlaug laughed and tilted his head back, but not long enough to be distracted and looked at Faolan with more hate in his eyes than Faolan had ever seen in a creature before. "Do you really think Roanus acted solely on revenge towards the Guardians?" That got Faolan's attention. "Ah, I see you do...or should I say, you did?" Borlaug smirked antagonizing and looked down, shuffling his feet and shaking his head, once again gloating that he had something on Faolan. It was long enough and Faolan was on him faster than he realized. He tackled the Changeling and with a loud gurgle, Borlaug hit the ground with such a force his head bounced twice off the ground. Faolan clutched his throat and held him in place.

"No matter what delusions you may be entertaining, you will leave the child alone, or you will die." Faolan's face was inches from the creatures and he could feel his hot breath, labored from the pressure around his neck.

"Ah, the typical answer for anything that might stand in the Baelian's way; death. Doesn't it get old, Faolan, to follow so blindly in your father's footsteps? Do you not wish to have a voice of your own?" he choked out.

Faolan's grip tightened and Borlaug's face pinched in pain. "I see, so you have chosen death?" Faolan used his other hand and reached down to grab the dagger. Borlaug kicked his feet out causing Faolan to shift enough that the creature was able to wiggle his way out of Faolan's grip and roll away, coughing. Faolan got up, grabbing the dagger and lunged after the Changeling. He dove for large bush, trying to get Faolan to follow him, hoping that it would distract him enough to be able to get back to the child, but Faolan, instead of following, went and stood against the house, leaning his back against the child's window.

"Try as you might, young elf, I will finish my task tonight. You are only prolonging the inevitable." Borlaug lifted himself out of the bush and stood directly in front of Faolan, hoping to show an authoritative stance. He knew the worst would be to show fear.

"That is where you are desperately wrong. Faineth and her family are safe and so shall this child be. The only thing that is being prolonged is your miserable life. Please come here so we can end it quickly," Faolan's smile was wicked, but Borlaug wasn't bothered by it. Hatred for his kind was nothing new and neither were death threats. It was part of the job description. No one had ever handed him a child willingly. He laughed at Faolan's words and just how wrong he really was.

"Safe? You really think they are safe?" He laughed harder, almost buckling over. "My dear, sweet, stupid prince, by now they are all dead."

The heat from anger rose in Faolan until the world around him turned red. "That's impossible."

"It's improbable, maybe, but not necessarily impossible. You see, that's the part of the plan you didn't hear. Roanus followed your sweet Ennon when he crossed back over. He should have reached the safe house yesterday, completing the extinction of your friends," the creature boasted. "His plan to gain the crown will be complete with the only threat out of the way, it will be easy for him to attain."

Faolan mulled over the possibility of the reality of Borlaug's words and thought he had to be bluffing to catch him off guard. Collecting himself and returning his thoughts to the present situation he let his worry slip away. "I won't fall for your tricks again."

"Tricks, is it? I see that even the truth is wasted on you. Maybe Roanus should have gotten rid of his family, instead of the Guardians. Maybe then we could live in peace," Borlaug hissed and made the mistake of looking down again. Faolan's anger grew and without thinking, he lunged at the Changeling, sinking the dagger deep into its chest. Borlaug's eyes grew wide for a few seconds and he tried to say something but all that came out was a raspy hiss as his lungs filled with blood. His eyes grew heavy and with a final sigh, he went still. Faolan lifted his dagger out of his chest and Borlaug's lifeless body fell to the earth, vanishing before he hit the ground.

Faolan took a few steps back, looking around, wondering where he had gone. A barn owl hooting above shook his attention off the area below and he looked to the sky. In what little time they had fought, the clouds had cleared, making way for a spectacular display of stars. He looked around once more, letting the heaviness of the situation sink in and sighed with relief that Borlaug was really gone. Maybe he had used a charm to make sure he returned to the other realm if something like this had happened. Faolan wasn't that educated fully in all aspects of magic, since the possibilities and abilities were almost endless and differed between species, it could have been possible. Still, the situation didn't sit well with him and not knowing for sure if he would be back, or if he wasn't, in fact, truly dead, he refocused himself and headed for the window.

23. Class Dismissed

Breakfast had been hurried with little to no conversation since Lady Breaga wanted to squeeze in as much training as she could with Faineth before Hattie was expected to arrive to retrieve her. Leaving the dishes to be dealt with later, the three headed outside into the crisp morning air. Faineth shivered the minute she stepped foot out of the castle and onto the field that lay to the side. The sun was just barely rising on the horizon and she noticed an odd, darkly pinkish fog had settled and she stopped to observe it, causing Willow to bump into the backs of her legs.

With the intensity of the training, Lady Breaga insisted the skirts had to go and after mumbling a few words, Faineth watched as her skirts started to shake and billow and with a sudden pop, they disappeared. In their place were the oddest looking bottoms she had ever seen. Similar to Ennon's, but not quite the same, they were made of thick leather and shorter and tighter than something her brother would wear and they made her look five stones smaller. "One cannot achieve greatness dressed for a ball," Breaga had laughed, but now seeing how much easier it allowed her to maneuver around, she wondered if she would ever go back to the layer upon layer of skirts that most Guardian women wore. Probably not and she smiled with the thought of the look on her mother's face when she would return home dressed like her brother.

"Not sure I have ever seen fog this color before," she said, turning her thoughts back to the odd weather.

"It is usually a sign that tragedy has happened, but this time I think it's because we expect Hattie's return soon," Lady Breaga mocked. "Pick up the pace, child! I have much to cover today and since it is my last with you, you need to pay attention," she continued then turned to look directly at Faineth. "Especially if you want to see my horses," she added.

Faineth picked up the pace, shortening the distance between them in seconds and smiled as she joined her new mentor as they headed in the direction of the flat, even field they had used to train since her arrival. Even though Lady Breaga talked as if this was the only time they would have together, Faineth had already decided a few days ago, that this would not be the last time she spent learning from Lady Breaga. Not only did she want to embrace more of the magic side of her people, thinking that it would help if they (specifically her family) were ever under attack again, but also she desperately wanted to know of this great grandmother that she was supposed to be so much like. She wondered why her mother hadn't talked about her much, but then wondered if it was because Olorin's own mother, Edin, hadn't known much herself, because Clairn had died when Edin had been born.

The fog was thinner now and she could see her surroundings a bit more easily, but it still had an eeriness to it. "Could it be a delay with what happened with my people?" she asked a few moments later.

"Could what be a delay? Please, Faineth, above all else, speak with sense. I'm not much into riddles this morning," Lady Breaga hissed, obviously already thinking of something else.

"I mean about the fog. You said it usually meant tragedy. Could it be delayed, the strange fog, I mean," Faineth corrected.

"No, dear. This is not a delay for what you and your people went through. This is the second fog I have seen since then; the first the day Roanus and his men attacked. This is something else," she answered, her voice softer than before. Faineth looked back towards Lady Breaga and noticed she too had a look of worry on her face. "We best get to work," she said, snapping out of the daze the fog had momentarily put her in.

Faineth followed obediently, but could let the subject die. "Do you suppose it is related?" She was worried about her family now, people she had realized she hadn't given a second thought to since she had left the safe house less than a week ago and found herself hoping they were alright.

"Related?" Lady Breaga stopped and turned, bringing her full attention back to Faineth. "No, dear, I do not. I do, however, see the worry on your face and now question your focus today." Lady Breaga closed the gap between them and placed her hands on Faineth's shoulders. Warmth washed through Faineth and she felt her whole body relax. "Now, then, shall we continue?" Faineth shook her head, but not to say no and quickly nodded so that she would not give Lady Breaga the wrong idea.

"Sorry, your Ladyship," Faineth sighed, realizing her questions would go unanswered.

"Your *Ladyship*? For heaven's sake, child! I am not the Queen!" Lady Breaga laughed.

"Sorry," Faineth replied. Her head felt foggy and wondered if Lady Breaga's hands carried more than a comforting gesture.

"So many apologies for someone who has done nothing wrong," Taking a step back and placing her hands on her hips, Lady Breaga cocked her head to one side and sighed. "Tell you what, we get through this morning's teachings and I promise to look into what the meaning behind the fog is. Deal?"

"Deal," Faineth answered suddenly both anxious and afraid of what she would discover. Following closely behind her teacher, Faineth's head started to clear and she was now thinking of the many possibilities of what could be the reason behind the fog. Had they caught Roanus? Even if they had, the only thing that could justify a tragedy would be if the King had him executed and she didn't see that happening. Even if what he did was terrible, she knew the King and his kindness. No, she could see him banished before he would ever see him killed. Had he escaped and destroyed the remaining dragons? When she and Hattie were on top of the tower, she could see many still okay and that was just a few days ago, but the fog was happening now, so it could have happened, couldn't it? The only thought with any logic to it, was that somehow Roanus had escaped and had gotten to the remaining dragons, or worse…her family. Her head throbbed as if her blood was actually boiling.

"Lady Breaga! Stop!" Faineth yelled out, having fallen further behind her teacher than she had thought. She knew she would not be able to accomplish anything without knowing.

"By the Makers gifts, what is it, child?" Lady Breaga yelled back, clearly frustrated in her student. She started to approach Faineth again with her arms raised, but Faineth stopped her with a raised hand.

"Please do not belittle me by calming me with persuasive magic again. I need to know what is going on, not be pacified so that I can learn another trick," she shouted, her voice showing her growing anger. "I need to know if my family is..." Faineth would have finished, but an odd whooshing and clanking sound interrupted her thoughts. The two women on the field looked to the sky simultaneously just as what looked like a flying lion with a large beak carrying and enormous amount of fabric on its back, swooped down from the clouds. Faineth looked at it, puzzled as it appeared to be both in control and as if it were going to crash land at the same time. "What is..."

From above them came shouts from a voice Faineth recognized immediately. Lady Breaga sighed and lowered her head, shaking it back and forth, in what looked like disgust.

"Oh. yay, she's early," she complained.

"Breaga! Faineth! I have grave news! Glad I found ye both together! Saves me time, really," Hattie lectured as she landed, to Faineth's surprise, rather gracefully. The large creature made her look even smaller than the Wood Gnome already was and the two women watched as she clumsily dismounted. Faineth wondered if it might have been an easier task if she too had a pair of what Lady Breaga called "britches" instead of the layers upon layers of skirts. After both feet finally touched the ground, she adjusted those skirts, including pulling a few layers back over her head and stood up and heaved a heavy sigh, regaining her composure. The large creature took three large steps back to give her ample room, folded its wings, and sat on its hind quarters. Hattie, who looked as if she had been crying, ran towards Faineth and Lady Breaga.

"Oh, thank the stars in heaven above, I've found you both!" she shouted, out of breath.

"Yes, yes, you mentioned that already," Lady Breaga answered sounding irritated.

Hattie ignored her and took a moment to look Faineth over, raising her eyebrows in question when she got to the legs part of the examination, said a quick "huh," then regained her composure, continuing on as if she hadn't taken a short break. "There's trouble brewing and I need to get her back," she added, talking directly to Lady Breaga now.

"What sort of trouble? Really, Hattantia, it couldn't wait? I still had a few more things I feel are vital for her to learn, besides you're early, and I was going to show her my hor-" Lady Breaga complained, speaking so fast it took Hattie a few seconds to interrupt.

"Stuff your arrogance in yer britches, Breaga! This child is needed back at Castle Baelian and the sooner, the better!" Hattie retorted loudly, her accent rolling off her tongue like thunder. Although she was half Lady Breaga's size, she well made up for it in spirit. Lady Breaga's features softened a bit and Faineth could almost see her swallow her pride.

"Fine, but I get her back when whatever it is she is needed for is finished and I get to keep her as long as I want," the Lady countered, once again standing her ground. As much as Faineth feared what had brought Hattie all worked up over, riding whatever that thing was, she wasn't blind to the fact that Breaga was fighting for time with her.

"It's a Griffin, dear," Hattie answered her thoughts. "I'll introduce you later. As for now, we really need to get you back. The Queen herself, the dear, has asked for you personally."

"Anya wants Faineth?" Lady Breaga asked, her voice giving away her surprise over who wanted Faineth. Her anger completely dissolved with a nod of Hattie's head and she grabbed Faineth's arm and headed back towards her home.

"Where on her life are ye off to now?" Hattie shouted.

Lady Breaga stopped and turned towards Hattie, some of the indifference towards Hattie returning. "She'll need her things," she continued in a sarcastic tone, as if Hattie was really quite stupid to have asked in the first place.

Hattie, reacting with what Faineth was sure to be equal sarcasm, began to yell. "We don't have time for that, you fool! She is fine the way she is! She can come back for her things later. Now, Faineth, you can leave the rest of those weapons with Breaga, but maybe keep that smaller dagger. Looks handy enough without being too clunky."

She quickly mounted the creature, which had already lain down to accommodate Hattie's size, then waited for Faineth to climb on behind her. Faineth quickly dropped everything and tucked the small dagger Hattie had told her to keep in her belt and sprinted towards the Griffin, making her mount look like an art. Hattie smirked.

"And here I thought ye didn't know how to do that," she half giggled, placing her un-used hand that she had extended out for Faineth to grab back on the strap that was buried under the fur that surrounded the animal's neck. She motioned for Willow to sit between them and after tucking her in, making sure she wasn't going to fall off, the Griffin stood up. It extended its wings out and with one large flap, it took to the air. Faineth corrected her seating to feel more secure and by the time she realized she hadn't yet said goodbye to Lady Breaga, they were already high above the tallest peak of her home. She looked down at the woman, standing alone and waved.

"No worries, dear. If all is well, you'll be seeing that...*woman* again," Hattie spoke her name with disdain and it made Faineth wondered what had happened between the two to cause such disgust in each other, "soon enough."

"Hattie, what's this all about, anyways?" Faineth leaned forward so that she could hear her better. They were up high enough now that the wind and the whooshing of wings were making it hard to hear clearly.

"Hang tight. We've a long way to go in a short time, mind ye, and you'll be knowin' the whys to your whats in due time," Hattie yelled back. She gave a slight nudge to the animal's side and the Griffin shot into the morning sky faster than any dragon Faineth had ever ridden.

24. A New Life

"My brother did what?" yelled Faineth. She was pacing back and forth in the front of a very large fireplace in an even larger room that the King and Queen would accept guests in. It was large enough to house at least one third the men in the royal guard, but all it contained now was Faineth and Queen Anya. "Of all the… seriously…disastrous…stupid ideas! What was he thinking? Oh, I know! He wasn't!" her shouting continued and Anya, deciding this might go on a bit, sat down in one of the chairs positioned next to the fire. Willow too, deciding she had had enough with trying to follow Faineth back and forth, went and curled up next to the fire.

The large door at the other end of the room opened and a strange person, or at least what Faineth thought was a person when she would get around to noticing him, entered the room carrying a very large tray, so large that all you could see was his stubby legs that wobbled as he walked and the top half of his hat. He walked over towards the Queen and set the large tray down beside her on the small table next to the chair. A large teapot, two cups, and a plate with enough biscuits to feed Faineth's family for a week adorned the top of the tray. Faineth was still pacing and still yelling about Ennon, so the small man took a step back, noticed a dragon by the fire and raised one eyebrow in question.

"Oh, thank you, Palfred. You are most kind and understanding," said the Queen, dismissing his inquiry about Willow, drawing his attention back to her.

"T'wasn't me, mum, the King sent me in. Said you might be a while. I think he didn't want you getting hungry," Palfred said in a low gravelly voice, nodding his head towards the large plate of biscuits. His eyes lingered on them a few seconds longer and seeing this, Anya offered one to him, as well. "Well, if you insist, mum," he answered and bent at the knee slightly, in a thankful curtsy. Faineth, finally smelling the tea, looked over and saw that they indeed had company.

"Oh, hello," she said and looked at Anya in surprise. "My apologies, I didn't hear you come in."

"Neither did the folk down the hall," Palfred teased, but Anya shushed him.

"Faineth, this is Palfred. Palfred, this is Faineth. She's just been told some news that has turned out to be rather disturbing to her. Let's not make light of it," the Queen scolded.

"Sorry, mum, sorry, Milady," he said, doing the bent-kneed curtsy towards Faineth this time. Faineth smiled, thinking that the sight of him was rather silly. He was somewhat like Hattie and the other Wood Gnomes, but shorter and more rugged looking. Almost as if they had been caught in a tidal wave and spit out to dry on the sand for a month. He had deep set wrinkles and a large, much too large for his face, nose that extended out far past the length of his chin. His eyes were beady but kindly and his eyebrows looked as if Faineth's mother could braid them, long and wiry. His clothes looked clean but worn, like they were a part of him, and his shoes matched his hat, both large and very pointy at the ends. His hands were large and small wiry hairs, that matched his eyebrows, grew out from each knuckle. His ears grew out beyond what Faineth knew to be normal length and pointed at the tip and his hair matched his eyebrows and knuckles, only it looked to be tied back, at least she assumed, not having seen the back of him yet.

"I'm sorry, what are you?" Faineth looked at him curiously, but could tell instantly Palfred had taken it as an insult and thought she better explain herself. "It's just that I haven't had the chance to meet too many, uh…new people yet," she said with pinched brow, hoping he would accept it. "Are you related to Hattie's people?"

"Hattie's people? You mean Hattantia? No, mum, I am not a Wood gnome. I'm a Brownie, mum," and with that, he stood two inches taller. He was obviously very proud with his heritage.

"Well, Palfred, it's very nice to meet you," Faineth added. "I just realize I have yet a lot to learn."

"Well, mum, if rumors are true, I'll say you have learned a lot already. Many apologies about your situation, mum."

"Thank you, Palfred," Faineth answered, softening to him instantly. He was as different in appearance and attitude as black was to white. Where one was harsh, the other was soft.

"Welcome, mum." He turned and looked to Anya. "Will that be all, mum?"

"Yes, Palfred, thank you," she said with a smile.

"Welcome, mum," he said again and turned and shuffled out of the room, this time leaving the tray, but not without a second glance towards Willow, only this time, he smiled.

"He's been with my family since before I was born," Anya said in almost a whisper.

"How old is he?" Faineth asked almost choking on her biscuit. "And why haven't I seen him before?"

"He will be four hundred and eighty two on his next birthday and he was with his family celebrating his Uncle's birthday."

"How long ago was that?" Faineth asked, fully knowing in all the times she had been here before, she had never stumbled up on him.

"Eight years ago," Anya said nonchalantly. "Brownies live for a very long time, so they only celebrate a birthday every twenty five years and the parties can last, well, years," she giggled. "He hadn't been to one in so long that Carrig insisted he go this time. I'm so glad he did. He came back looking happier than I had seen him since I was a child." She sighed then straightened up, set her cup of tea down and looked at Faineth. "You mustn't be upset at

Ennon. I know he did what he thought to be right and now I tend to believe it was, too."

"But the risk," Faineth argued and sat down on the chair facing Anya.

"Is over," Anya answered. "Word has it he is back and it is done. He has promised he won't be crossing over again."

"It's done; does that mean it actually worked?"

"It appears so," Anya said, patting Faineth on the knee. "Now we wait and when the time is right, we will see about an introduction."

"And they're safe, but what about Roanus?" Faineth asked, having gotten the full story of what had happened with him when she had first arrived.

"Although he is still unaccounted for, Faolan has seen to their safety personally, my dear, and we know Faolan. They will be alright," the queen tried to reassure her, but Faineth's worry wasn't budging. Even with the news of Ennon and her new family member and of Roanus escaping, it still didn't explain that eerie fog she had seen this morning while she was with Lady Breaga.

"But, Milady, this morning at Lady Breaga's," she went to explain, but Anya cut her off.

"How is that old crow, anyway?" she laughed. "Oh, the fun we used to have. I sure do miss your great grandmother," she sighed. "You know, Faineth, the older you get, the more you look just like her."

"So I've been told," she answered shortly, reaching down to feel the outline of the photograph proving Queen Anya's words in her pocket. "But this morning,"

"Did you also know that your great grandmother was one of the most powerful witches of her kind?"

"Lady Breaga may have mentioned that, too, yes," she answered politely, but getting frustrated that no one seemed to listen to her anymore.

"Well, she was. She truly was," Queen Anya continued, resting back into her chair, her eyes taking on a faraway look, as if she was heavy in thought. Faineth sighed.

"Your Highness," she started and Anya's attentions were back on her. "This morning, there was a strange mist, like a fog," she paused when the Queen's expression didn't change as if hearing about a fog was not unusual. "Lady Breaga said it only happened in times of tragedy.

This got the Queen's attention. Sitting straight up in her chair, she leaned towards Faineth. "Tell me, child, what color was it?"

"It was really strange, unlike anything I had seen before, almost like the color of old blood," Faineth answered and Anya gasped. She stood without another word to Faineth and pulled a large rope near the fireplace. A few seconds later, the doors flew open and two of the King's guard entered as if they had run the whole way.

"Yes, Milady?" one of them asked.

"What news have you from Faolan?" she asked and Faineth noticed she had a ring of panic to her tone.

"We've just had word that the Changeling was killed, Milady, and Faolan and the child are now safe," the other guard answered and Faineth wondered what a Changeling was.

"So then what?" she said in almost a whisper. As if she had suddenly realized something, she turned and looked to Faineth in horror. Clasping her hand to her mouth, she turned back towards the guards.

"Has anyone, and I mean anyone, heard from the R'yor's today?"

The moment her family's name left the Queens lips, Faineth's knees grew weak and she fell back into the chair she had stood from the minute the guards had entered the room. The Queen and the two guards continued to talk, but none of it made any sense to Faineth. Her mind was fuzzy, almost as if she was about to faint and she laid her head back in the chair and closed her eyes. She knew earlier that it had to be tied to her family and now Queen Anya's fears told her she was right. She looked down as she felt Willow crawl up in her lap, trying to bring her some comfort and she felt the first of the many tears to come fall. Her hearing began to clear just as the Queen was ordering her to stay put and turn to give new orders, which she thought included sending the knights to the safe house to check on her family, to the men standing next to her. There were four total now and Faineth wondered when the other two had shown up. They were nodding their heads in agreement and they all, Queen Anya included, turned and exited the room, leaving Faineth and Willow alone.

Willow, a little larger now, placed her head on the side of Faineth's and gave it a nudge and Faineth frowned. Willow looked at her again and placed her chin under Faineth's and this time, lifted her face up. Faineth realized she was trying to help her snap out of the haze and shook her head on her own. Willow almost looked as if she smiled and jumped off her lap and motioned towards the door.

"Right," Faineth agreed. She got up and ran to the door to check and see if they had been locked in, but it opened for her. She peered out into the hall and saw that they were truly alone. "Okay, Willow, we need to get back to that house without being seen. Got any suggestions?"

Willow turned and went back into the room they had been in and went to one of the windows and made a few head gestures telling Faineth she wanted it opened. She followed instruction without hesitation and before she could wonder what her little friend was up to, Willow leaned her head out and let out a loud cry that made Faineth cover her ears.

"I said without being seen, that also meant heard," she scolded, but out of the corner of her eye, she saw a large shadow from above and when she looked up, a huge smile spread across her face. "Willow! You're a genius!"

Willow returned her compliment with a soft bellow and the two of them readied themselves and when the time was right, leapt from the window and onto the massive back of a Mountain Wyvern. Faineth yelled out an order and the massive dragon took off in the direction of the safe house, she then grabbed the whistle Hattie had given her and blew into it with all her breath. She knew these dragons even though she had little time actually spent with them. She knew they were fast and steady and above all loyal and if Roanus was anywhere near the safe house, this dragon would eat well. Faineth smiled wickedly at the thought of Roanus' demise if they were to catch him, but it didn't pacify the hurt and worry she was feeling for her family and she prayed they would make it in time.

As they flew along, her thoughts were with her brother and what he had done. With what they were facing now, the anger she had felt earlier was gone. To imagine life without her people was one thing, but to imagine it without her family was a whole other thing. A void so large started to grow in the pits of her stomach and shadows were passing by her so quickly that she thought for a moment she was either going to be sick or going to pass out again, so she laid her body against the dragon's back and turned her head to one side. With weary eyes, she looked out at the horizon, but what she saw caused her to sit up with a jolting speed. Dragons, of all shapes and sizes, flew along beside them. She looked to the other side and behind them as well and finding even more dragons, she was able to smile between the tears. She had never seen so many, not even when she was atop the tower with Hattie. There had to be almost fifty dragons. They were flying all around them, weaving in and out of pattern, dipping under and over the one she was riding and watching all of it was dizzying.

A larger shadow crept over her, while she was looking below and she slowly looked up, having a feeling of despair. An even more massive, jet black dragon flew directly above her and she was instantly afraid. She had heard many stories of the infamous Black Dragons but had yet to ever see one, especially this close and she had no idea what to expect. For all she knew, the large creature could swoop down and claim her as dinner. The dragon lowered its head and looked directly at her without flying off course. A feeling of cold came over her, but with it came a feeling of peace. A low humming sound rang in her ears and after a few seconds the dragon above her grew impatient and bellowed loudly. Faineth clasped her ears, but the humming didn't stop. It grew louder. She shook her head to try and make it stop, but it wouldn't. The sound started to change pitch and the loudness waivered, almost like she was going in and out of a tunnel. Then, as if it had been there all along, muffled words intertwined with the humming, started to call out to her. She heard 'Guardian' first, but it was slurred, then she thought she heard the word 'safety', but that, too, was slurred. The humming grew so loud that she shook her head in pain and looked up. The dragon was back to staring straight at her and it bellowed at her this time. Just as it started, the humming stopped and she could hear the words clearer now.

"I will get you there safely, Guardian," the words in her mind said and she looked back up to the dragon overhead.

"Was that you?" she yelled and the creature nodded. Faineth couldn't help but smile and she looked to Willow, who had been flying beside them for a while. "Say something," she yelled.

"I love you," answered Willow in her mind. Faineth felt her heart twist, but not in a painful way, more in a swelling sort of way, after something gets so full it might burst. Warm tears slid down her cheeks.

"I love you, too," she answered softly, but knew Willow could hear her because at that precise moment, the small dragon rolled in the air.

"It will be okay, Faineth," Willow whispered in her thoughts. "No matter what we find, it will be alright."

"I hope so, little one, I hope so," she answered.

The Black Dragon swooped down in front of them and then dropped; allowing the dragon Faineth was riding to fly directly over it. As soon as they passed, the giant dragon then spread its wings wide and angled them back in a way that it herded the rest of the dragons behind him, forcing them to fly in formation, instead of random chaos. Faineth was grateful and yelled thank you to the Black Dragon, something she never expected to do in her life time. It was odd enough to be flying alongside of one, let alone having a conversation with one. But to be actually thankful that it was here, with her, keeping her safe, that was what she never dreamed would happen. All the things she had grown to believe about them had obviously been wrong and a slight pang of guilt crossed her, but she quickly released it and refocused on what was waiting for them.

The Black Dragon, flying the opposite side of Willow, lowered his head as if bowing to her. "You're welcome."

"Do you have a name?" shouted Faineth.

"My name is Bade. There are only three of us left," he answered. "You are our Guardian now, Faineth."

The weight of his words was heavy. She and her family, if they were still alive (thinking that gave her an awful ache, deep inside) were the only Guardians left. It was truly up to them now to assure the safety and wellbeing of these wondrous creatures. Faineth tried to let that sink in for a moment but was quickly distracted as she started to recognize her surroundings.

"We're almost there," she shouted up at Bade. "You must stay safe, no matter what," she added.

"We won't leave this for you to handle alone, Guardian," Bade argued, in a way that told Faineth he would not change his mind.

"Fine, but please, stop calling me Guardian. My name is Faineth."

"Alright, Faineth, we will be at your side."

"Thank you, Bade," she smiled and wondered how many more times she would thank him before the day's end.

Still in formation, the group dipped down lower and circled the safe house before landing, forming a large circle around the house. Faineth quickly dismounted the dragon she had ridden over on the minute it crouched down and ran towards the front door.

"Faineth! Stop!" yelled Willow in her mind. " What if he is still in there?"

She stopped just in front of the door and turned. "What if they are in danger? I can't wait!" Turning back around, she barged into the small house and made it four steps in before she saw her father's feet extending out of the kitchen.

"No!" she screamed and ran to him, dropping down to his side. She lifted his head, cradled it to her chest and started to rock back forth, sobbing uncontrollably. "Father…no…" she choked.

Willow poked her head in through the door and seeing Faineth and her father, let out a bellow behind her, letting the others know of their demise. One by one, the dragons started to bellow. The sight would have been truly something to see if Faineth hadn't been so upset over her father's death. She hugged him tightly, then after what seemed an eternity she laid him back down on the floor and left him to look for her mother. She found Olorin towards the back of the house in the back bedroom, the one Faineth had used. She was propped up against the bed holding a shirt of Faineth's to her chest. She looked as if she had been frozen solid, but the blood running from her ears told a different story; one of death by magic. The look of fear on her face would be one Faineth would never forget. Fresh tears raced down her cheeks and guilt washed over her for not being here for them.

"If you had been, then you would have suffered the same fate," Willow said, having come in behind her. "There's nothing left for us here."

"Ennon! Where's Ennon?" she asked weakly. She had looked in every room on her way back to this one and he wasn't in any of them. "Did you check outside?"

"Yes, but no one else is here. Maybe he got away. We need to go before Roanus comes back with more men. If he hears of us being here, I'm afraid that's exactly what he will do." Willow pleaded with her.

"How did he ever find this place?" she questioned, looking back at her mother. "I can't just leave them, Willow," Faineth cried, but even she knew they weren't really there anymore. Willow walked over to her and leaned into her. She dropped her hand and rested it on her back. The two stood in silence for a while. How could this have happened? She had completely failed them. "Help me get them outside. I'll not let them go without a proper burial."

"Alright, but we really need to hurry. I have a bad feeling and I know the others feel the same."

It took a while for the two of them to get Olorin and Arien properly buried, but when they had finished, Faineth placed cuttings of her mother's favorite vine on the graves and said a prayer of passing. It was a surreal moment for her as they walked away and headed back around to the front of the house. The dragons were haphazardly gathered in the field next to the house, waiting for them to finish. As Faineth walked toward them, her heart sank. She had lost her parents and had no idea where Ennon was or if he was still alive. She had no clue where to even begin looking for him and then what? What if she did find him, would he be alive? If he was, what was their future now?

She was completely alone other than the dragons that now surrounded her and how was she to tend to all of them alone? She hadn't even seen half of them before, let alone know what species they were or what their needs would be. And where were they to go? It's not like any village or city would be accepting them with open arms, with clean beds and a warm meal. Her head hung in defeat as the dragons circled her, creating a barrier of protection around her. One of the dragons slowly approached her and dropped a large package at her feet.

"What's this," she asked looking up.

"It's from the Queen," answered the mid-sized olive colored dragon, Faineth recognized as one that belonged to the Western Clans.

Faineth opened it and inside was a map. She looked at it closer and it appeared to lead to a large stone archway within a grouping of trees not far from the location of the safe house. A note attached to the map caught her eye.

Faineth,

If you are able to remain safe, we have set up a place for you and the dragons to live safely. It isn't the Mountains you grew up in, but it's comfortable and the land is rich. I know you will be able to make a good home for you and the dragons there. Please get there as fast as you can upon reading this. I don't know what Roanus is up to, but I don't trust him at all anymore. I think he is truly mad. Anya and I will be the only ones that know of your survival and location. It is imperative we keep it this way. Not even Faolan can know. Send word of your arrival with the dragon that gave you this. He knows the way back and how to stay hidden.

All our love,

Carrig and Anya

She slowly folded the note back up and tucked it into the pocket of her shirt and wondered quietly how on earth they had gotten this to her when she had only left a short while ago. Tears streamed down her face and again she faced the question: could she do this?

"If I may," Bade interrupted, "I think I know the answer to that question you just asked yourself. You're allowed to scream and you're allowed to cry, but you are not allowed to give up,"

At that very moment, she decided to never live a sheltered life again and never let life shatter her. She knew that she needed to learn everything there was to know about Ethreal and what it truly meant to be a Dragon Guardian. Her life and the lives of the dragons depended on it.

"Follow me," she ordered and turned and looked at the house one last time and said a silent goodbye. She looked to the dragons closest to her and gave a weak smile and headed in the direction of their new home according to the map. She could make out the trees in front of them so she knew it wouldn't take long to get there. Twenty minutes later, they were collectively gathered in front of a massive stone arch, one that would easily allow Bade to pass under without struggle.

"It's a portal," Faineth whispered.

"Do you know the magic to use one?" Bade asked.

Faineth turned to see him towards the back of the group. "Ever the protector" she thought and smiled. "We don't need one. All one has to do is walk through it."

The dragons' thoughts were racing through her mind and she found herself wishing she couldn't hear them again, if for only a short time. All those voices at once were almost painful. The pain of losing her parents was still strong in her mind as well and the two combined was becoming unbearable.

"Please," she shouted, raising her hands in the air. "I know you are all scared and well, I am, too. But I know the Queen and King. They are good people and would never do anything to hurt us. It's just us now and we have no other choice. If we stay, then we risk death and I'm not ready to do that." She sighed. She was sure the depravity of her situation would hit her soon, but now she was just numb. Numb to her feelings of complete despair and fear. Fear that she is never going to get to argue with her mother again or fish with her father. Fear that she would never be able to find Ennon and fear that she was the last of her kind outside of a babe she had yet to meet. The dragons had begun to settle a bit and she gathered herself together once more.

"Let's just go and see it. If nothing else, we can stay for a while and let things settle and if it doesn't suit us, we can always come back later. Just give it a chance. I can't lose all of you as well," she choked out. Willow walked up to her and dipped her head under Faineth's hand and looked up at her.

"We would never leave you, Faineth," the small dragon said reassuringly and turned and walked through the portal, disappearing into the other side. Faineth looked up at the rest and followed Willow and one by one, the rest of the dragons followed her, until the last one, Bade, dipped his large head and disappeared behind them. The second his tail was out of sight, the ground began to rumble and the rock arch began to shake. The solid rock started to liquefy and within minutes, had completely evaporated into thin air, leaving no trace, as if it never existed.

~*~

He quietly closed the window behind him and turned softly as to not disturb her. Walking softly over to the crib, he bent down to look at her sleeping and his wings brushed the mobile that hung from above it, causing it to make a twinkling sound. He look up and grabbed it before it could make any more sound and he quickly looked back at the baby, now directly under him. She stirred and sighed, but remained asleep. He smiled and looked back up to the mobile and saw that it was made up of five tiny fairies, all dressed in what looked like dresses made from large green leaves and he giggled.

"Now, if only Aisling could see this," he joked, knowing full well that she would think it an insult to her race. He looked

216

back down and saw that the baby had indeed awoken to his voice and was smiling up at him. "Well, hello there, little one."

He scooped her up into his arms and went back over to the window to check to make sure Borlaug hadn't returned or had sent help and seeing nothing but the fields that surrounded the house, he went to sit in the chair that was in the opposite corner of the room. It moved under him and he was startled a bit, but after easing into it, he saw that its motion was gentle and only rocked back and forth. Noticing that it comforted the baby, he relaxed into it, rocking her.

"My name is Faolan and I have been sent here to protect you," he spoke softly and she cooed back at him, making him smile that much more. "You sure are a pretty one, aren't you? Looks like you got your auntie's hair," he noted, softly rubbing her flame red curls on the side of her head. Looking at her, he couldn't imagine anyone ever *wanting* to hurt a baby in the first place, let alone one so delicate. She truly was a gift. One that he hoped he could always be a part of.

A shadow crossed the window and he held her closer, feeling a slight panic of what was outside, but saw that it was just a large grey owl that had landed on a post. He knew this particular owl and smiled.

"Ah, Samson," he said, knowing the owl would hear him beyond the glass that separated them. "Let my father know I made it and she is safe now. Tell him I have defeated the Changeling," he added, not truly knowing that for sure, but sure enough to not worry anymore about it on this night. The owl took flight and disappeared into the night.

Faolan began to rock again and he hummed a soft tune he remembered from when he was a small child that his mother would sing to him. The baby started to fuss and Faolan grabbed a small silver rattle from his inside pocket and waved it over her. Two small dangling wings on either side of the middle piece danced and clinked and she settled down to watch it.

"I brought this just for you. It was mine when I was little and now you can have it as a reminder that I will always be here for you, my little Maggie. No one will try and hurt you ever again. You have my word."

He continued to hum and rock and after a few minutes she quietly fell back asleep peacefully settled in his arms.

The End.... Or is it?